FINDING THE EDGE

USA TODAY Bestselling Author

DEBRA WEBB

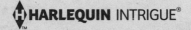

This book is dedicated to the outstanding men and women of
the Chicago Police Department. Thanks for all you do!

Recycling programs
for this product may
not exist in your area.

ISBN-13: 978-1-335-63915-8

Finding the Edge

Copyright © 2018 by Debra Webb

Printed in U.S.A.

Debra Webb is the award-winning *USA TODAY* bestselling author of more than one hundred novels, including those in reader-favorite series Faces of Evil, the Colby Agency and the Shades of Death. With more than four million books sold in numerous languages and countries, Debra's love of storytelling goes back to childhood on a farm in Alabama. Visit Debra at www.debrawebb.com.

Books by Debra Webb

Harlequin Intrigue

Colby Agency: Sexi-ER

Finding the Edge

Faces of Evil

Dark Whispers
Still Waters

**Colby Agency:
The Specialists**

Bridal Armor
Ready, Aim...I Do!

Colby, TX

Colby Law
High Noon
Colby Roundup

**Debra Webb writing
with Regan Black**

Harlequin Intrigue

*Colby Agency:
Family Secrets*

Gunning for the Groom

*The Specialists:
Heroes Next Door*

The Hunk Next Door
Heart of a Hero
To Honor and To Protect
Her Undercover Defender

Visit the Author Profile page at Harlequin.com.

CAST OF CHARACTERS

Todd Christian—He let Eva down once, but he's not the same man. He's here to stay this time to protect her from the drug lord who wants her dead.

Eva Bowman—Eva is a nurse. She heals people, and yet her actions took a man's life. Now his older brother wants her dead. Can she trust the man who once broke her heart to keep her safe?

Lena Bowman—Eva's sister is Chicago's most famous investigative journalist. How far will she go for the story?

Ian Michaels—Victoria's right hand at the Colby Agency.

Victoria Colby-Camp—The head of the prestigious Colby Agency.

Dr. Devon Pierce—A brilliant surgeon and the creator of the most state-of-the-art emergency room.

Miguel Robles—Will do anything to avenge his brother's death.

Chapter One

"We're going to need more gurneys!" Dr. Marissa Frasier shouted.

Someone amid the fray yelled that more gurneys were coming. They had nine new victims besides the dozen already in the ER. All bleeding, some worse than others. All had been shot and all were armed. And every damned one sported white T-shirts with an odd circle inside a circle in the center and wore black beanie caps. Their shouted threats echoed like thunder, inciting fear. Thank God most of the other patients had been checked in and were either already triaged and stable or had nonlife-threatening emergencies.

Eva Bowman might have considered it just another crazy Friday night looming toward a code black if not for the three cars that had screeched into the ER entrance with those new victims. Several armed men had barged in, waving automatic guns and demanding help for their friends. The three apparently in charge had forced everyone in the waiting room onto the floor and sent the entire ER staff, including the receptionist and the two registration specialists, outside to help their friends.

In all the commotion, Eva hoped someone had been able to alert the police. One of the security guards had been shot. He and the other guard had been restrained and left on the floor in the waiting room, blood pooling around the injured man. One of the gunmen stood over the small crowd, his scowl shifting from one to the other as if daring someone to give him a reason to start shooting. Eva wished she was more knowledgeable about the tattoos and colors worn by the different gangs in the Chicago area, though she couldn't readily see how knowing would help at the moment. For now, she did what she was told and prayed help would arrive soon.

Eva pushed an occupied gurney through the double doors, leaving the lobby behind. All the treatment rooms were full so she found a spot in the corridor and parked. She ripped open the shirt of her patient. Male.

Mid to late twenties. Hispanic. He was sweaty and breathing hard. He'd lost some blood from the bullet wound on his left side. Lucky for him the bullet appeared to have exited without much fanfare. Still, he was no doubt in serious pain. Whatever his pain level, he clutched his weapon and continued to bellow arrogantly at his friends as if a shot to the gut was an everyday occurrence. From what little she recalled of high school Spanish, he seemed to be claiming victory over whatever battle had occurred. If the group of wounded men who had been scattered on the asphalt in front of the ER doors were the winners, she hated to think what condition the losers were in. Didn't take much of a stretch to imagine they were in all probability dead.

An experienced registered nurse, Eva performed a quick assessment of her patient's vitals. Respiration and pulse were rapid. Though his skin was warm and moist, his color remained good. From all indications he was not critical, but there could be underlying issues she could not assess. He would need an ultrasound to ensure no organs were damaged, and the wound would need to be cleaned and sutured.

"Sir, can you tell me your name?"

The man stared at her as if she'd asked him

to hand over his weapon. She decided to move on to her next question. "On a scale of one to ten, ten being the worst you've ever suffered, can you tell me how much pain you're in?"

"Cero."

She sincerely doubted that was the case but if he wanted to play the tough guy, that was fine by her.

Over the next few minutes her patient as well as the others were sorted according to their needs and ushered on to the next level of care. Some were taken straight to operating rooms while others went on to imaging for additional assessment. One nurse and a doctor had been allowed to treat the patients in the lobby. Eva remained in the ER helping to attend to those who had arrived and were triaged and assigned treatment rooms before the gunmen arrived and took over. The armed patients who didn't require further care were mostly loitering around the corridor waiting for the return of their friends who'd been sent off to imaging or to the OR. What they didn't seem to realize was that those friends wouldn't be coming back to join them tonight.

One of the other nurses had whispered to Eva that Dr. Frasier had initiated the emergency assistance protocol. The police had been made aware that the ER was under siege or under duress of some sort and required law enforcement intervention.

Once before she had found herself in a similar situation. Time was necessary for the police to arrive and assess the situation, then they would send in SWAT to contain the problem. She hoped no one else was hurt during the neutralization and containment of the gunmen. So far she had hidden three weapons. Two from patients who'd been rushed to the OR and one from the guy not a dozen feet away who claimed he was in zero pain. His pain had apparently been so nonexistent that he hadn't realized his fingers had loosened on the 9 mm he'd been waving around when he first arrived.

Dr. Frasier noticed what Eva was up to and gave her a look of appreciation. No matter that she had removed and hidden three weapons—there were still six armed victims as well as the three armed and uninjured men who had taken over the ER. Thankfully, the thug who appeared to be the boss had allowed the injured guard to be treated for the bullet he'd taken. The guard's injury was not life threatening. He and his partner for the night were now both locked in the supply room.

Eva glanced at her watch. Approximately ten seemingly endless minutes had elapsed since the police were notified of their situation via the emergency protocol. SWAT would be rolling in soon. She didn't have to look outside to know that cops would have already taken crucial positions in the parking area.

All handheld radios and cell phones had been confiscated and tossed into a trash can—except for Eva's. The only reason the pat down conducted by the shortest of the three jerks who'd taken over the ER hadn't revealed her cell phone was because she didn't carry it in her pocket or in an armband. Eva kept hers in an ankle band made just for cell phones. Her last boyfriend had been an undercover cop and he'd shown her all sorts of ways to hide weapons and phones. If she'd been smart she would have carried a stun gun strapped to her other ankle the way he suggested.

They might still be together if he had been able to separate his work from his personal life. It was one thing to pretend to be someone else to catch the bad guys but entirely another to take on a separate persona for the purposes of cheating on your girlfriend.

Apparently the guys playing king of the ER weren't savvy enough to be aware that, like gun manufacturers, cell phone manufacturers thought of everything when it came to keeping phones close to users. Whatever the case, Eva was grateful her phone was still right where it was supposed to be. All she needed was an opportunity to use it. Knowing the situation inside would be incredibly useful for the police, particularly in determining how they made their grand entrance.

Her cell phone had vibrated about twenty times. Probably her sister, Lena. An investigative journalist at a local television station, Lena had no doubt heard about the trouble at the Edge. The best journalists had good contacts within Chicago PD and the Edge always had news. A Level I Trauma test unit challenging the approach to emergency medicine, the Edge was the only one of its kind in the nation.

Eva glanced toward the rear of the emergency department and the door that led into the main corridor that flowed into imaging and the surgery suite, winging off to the Behavioral Unit on the left and Administration to the right. Then she surveyed the ongoing activity between her and the double doors that opened into the lobby area. The man in charge and his cohorts were in deep conversation with the three other patients who hadn't been moved on to another level of care. Dr.

Frasier was suturing the wound of one while Dr. Reagan was doing the same with another. Kim Levy, a nurse and Eva's friend, was bandaging the third patient's closed wound.

Eva eased back a step and then another. Four more steps and she would be through the door and into the corridor beyond the emergency department. Slow, deep breaths. No sudden moves. Another step, then another, and she was out the door.

Eva whirled away from the softly closing door and ran to the ladies' room. She couldn't lock the door since it didn't have one—no one wanted a patient to lock him or herself in the bathroom. Inside there were, however, two stalls with slide locks.

She slipped into the second one and snapped the stall latch into place, then sat on the closed toilet lid and pulled her knees to her chest so no one coming in would see her feet. She tugged her cell phone from its holster at her ankle and saw four missed calls and six text messages from her sister. She didn't dare make a voice call so she sent a text to her sister and asked her to update the police on the situation inside the ER. Three uninjured gunmen. Four injured with guns, five others currently unarmed and in imaging or an OR. One injured guard. Both guards incapacitated.

A few seconds later, Lena told her to stay calm and to keep a low profile. Help was already on-site. Daring to relax the tiniest bit, Eva slid the phone back into its holster.

All she had to do was stay calm. Easy enough. She stepped off the seat.

The sound of the door opening sent fear exploding in her veins. She flushed the toilet, took a breath and exited the stall.

The man she thought to be in charge waited for her. He leaned against the door, the weapon in his hand lying flat against his chest. She decided that all the intruders were under thirty. This one looked to be early twenties. Though he appeared younger than the others, he was clearly the boss.

Eva steadied herself. "This is the ladies' room." She stared at him. "*Baño femenino*."

He laughed. "*Si*."

Oh crap. She squared her shoulders and took a step toward the door...toward him. "I need to be back out there helping your friends."

He shook his head. "There is plenty help already."

Eva swallowed back the scream mushrooming in her throat. There was no one to hear. This jerk was slightly taller than her five-seven. He was heavier and more muscled than her for sure, and a hell of a lot meaner. But she might be able to take him...*if not for the gun*.

As if he'd read her mind, he smiled and pointed the muzzle at her head. "On your knees, bitch."

The shaking started so deep inside her that she wondered how she remained standing, yet somehow she did. "The police are coming." The words shook, too, but she couldn't keep her voice steady if her life depended on it. Right now the ability to continue breathing might very well depend on her next word or move. "If you're smart, you'll tell your friends and you'll run. *Now*, while you still can."

He nodded, that nasty grin still stretched across his lips. "Yes," he agreed, the word sounding more like *des* with his thick accent.

Since he made no move to rush to his friends and warn them, her advice had clearly fallen on deaf ears. "So you don't care if you get caught?" She shrugged. "You want to go to prison? Then *you* can be somebody's bitch."

He charged toward her, pinned her to the counter of the row of sinks behind her. Of their own volition, her hands shot up in surrender. "Just trying to help you out. You…you don't want the police to show up and find you distracted. If you go now, they won't catch you."

She hoped like hell the guy had enough self-preservation instinct to realize she had a valid point.

"You talk a lot for a dead girl," he growled as he jammed the muzzle against her temple now. "You give me some of *that*—" he slid his free hand down her belly, forcing it between her thighs "—with no trouble and I'll be gone so fast you'll still be begging for more."

Trapped between him and the counter with his damned gun pointed at her brain, she couldn't move, didn't dare scream. Her heart flailed against her sternum. *Stay calm. Your fear makes him stronger.*

"Okay, okay." This close she smelled the whiskey on his breath, could fully comprehend just how inebriated he was. Bleary eyes. Slurred speech. No wonder he wasn't worried about the police. She drew in a shaky breath. *Play along until you come up with a better plan.* "What do you want?"

He laughed. "Suck me."

She nodded as she slowly lowered her hands. The muzzle bored into her skull a little harder as she reached for his fly. He was fully erect, bulging against his jeans. Bile rose in her throat as she unfastened the button, then lowered the zipper. She told herself over and over she had no choice as she reached into his open fly. He didn't have on any underwear so he was right there. She closed the fingers of her right hand around him while somehow managing to restrain the shudder of revulsion.

In hopes of putting off what he really wanted, her hand started to move. He made a satisfied sound, his eyes partially closing. "Oh, yeah, that's a good start."

She worked her hand back and forth faster and faster, felt his body tense. Watched his eyes drift completely shut.

Now or never.

Eva ducked her head, jammed her left shoulder into his gut and pushed with every ounce of her body weight. At the same time, she released his penis and grabbed his testicles and twisted as hard as she could.

He screamed.

The weapon discharged.

The mirror over the sinks shattered.

He grabbed at her; she twisted her upper body out of reach, spinning them both around. The muzzle stabbed at her chest; she leaned away from the gun and rammed into him even harder. Another shot exploded into the air as they both went down. His head hit the counter, making a solid *thump* as his neck twisted sharply. They crashed to the cold tile floor. The air grunted out of her lungs. Eva was still squeezing his balls when she realized he was no longer moving.

Disentangling herself from him, she scooted a few feet away. His eyes blinked, once, twice…he mumbled something she couldn't comprehend.

Eva scrambled to her feet and backed toward the door. She should reach for his weapon…she should grab it and run…

The door burst inward, almost knocking her on top of the man on the floor.

Another of the gunmen stared first at her and then at the man on the floor whose fly was flared open with his erect penis poked out.

Before Eva could speak the man grabbed her by the hair with his left hand and the gun in his right shoved into her face. "What did you do to him?"

Shaking so hard now she could hardly speak, she somehow managed to say, "He tried to rape me, so I pushed him away and he fell…he hit his head."

The man shoved her to the floor. She landed on her knees. "Help him," he snarled.

Eva moved closer to her attacker. His eyes were open but he didn't look at her. When she touched his neck to measure his pulse he mumbled but his words were unintelligible. Pulse was rapid. His body abruptly tensed. Seizure. *Damn.*

"We need to get him into the ER now." She pushed to her feet. "He may have a serious head injury."

The man grabbed her by the hair once more and jerked her face to his. "Do you know what you've done?"

A new stab of terror sank deep into her chest. "He attacked me. I was trying—"

"If he dies," he snarled, the muzzle boring into her cheek, "*you* die."

Suddenly the gun went upward. His arm twisted violently. A *pop* echoed in the room. Not a gunshot...a bone...

The man howled in agony. His body was hurled toward the floor. He landed on the unforgiving tile next to his friend.

Eva wheeled around, readied to scream but swallowed back the sound as she recognized Dr. Devon Pierce, the Edge creator and administrator.

"Check the corridor," he ordered. "If it's clear, go to my office and hide. I've got this."

The man on the floor scrambled to get up and Pierce kicked him hard in the gut.

When Eva hesitated, he snarled, "Go!"

She eased the bathroom door open and checked the corridor. Clear. She slipped out of the room, the door closed behind her, cutting of the grunts and awful keening inside. Her first instinct was to return to the ER to see if her help was needed there, but Dr. Pierce had told her to hide in his office. She didn't know what he was doing here but she assumed he was aware somehow of all that had happened. Perhaps the emergency protocol automatically notified him or maybe he had been in his office working late. Bottom line, he was the boss.

She hurried along the corridor, took a right into another side hall past the storeroom and the file rooms. Fear pounded in her veins as she moved into the atrium. Pierce's office was beyond the main lobby. She held her breath as she hurried through an open area. When she reached his secretary's office and the small, private lobby she dared to breathe, then she closed herself in his office. The desk lamp was on. Apparently Pierce had been in his office working. She reached for her cell.

Before she could put through a call to her sister, she heard rustling outside the door. The roar of her own blood deafening in her ears, Eva glanced quickly around the room. She had to hide. Fast!

With no other option she ducked under his desk, squeezed as far beneath it as she could, folding her knees up to her chin and holding herself tight and small.

A soft swoosh of air warned the door of the administrator's office had opened.

She held her breath.

The intruder—maybe Pierce, maybe a cop—moved around the room. She had no intention of coming out of hiding until she knew for certain. The sound of books sliding across shelves and frames banging against the wall clarified that the intruder was neither Pierce nor a cop. Footfalls moved closer to her position. She needed to breathe. She pressed her face to her knees and dared to draw in a small breath. Black leather shoes and gray trousers appeared behind the desk. Her eyes widened with the dread spreading inside her.

Definitely male.

The man dropped into the leather executive chair and reached for the middle drawer of the desk. His rifling through the drawer contents gave her the opportunity to breathe again. He moved on to the next drawer, the one on his right. More of that rummaging.

Then he reached lower, for the final drawer on that side. She prayed he wouldn't bend down any lower because he would certainly see her.

She held her breath again. He shifted to access the drawers on the other side, and his foot came within mere centimeters of her hip. He searched through the three remaining drawers. Then he stood. Sharp movement across the blotter pad told her he was writing something. Finally, he moved away from the desk.

The door opened and then closed.

Eva counted to thirty before she dared to move. She scooted from under the desk and scanned the room. She was alone. Thank God. The books and framed awards and photos on the once neatly arranged shelves lay scattered about. Her gaze instinctively dropped to the desk.

I know what you did.

The words were scrawled on the clean expanse of white blotter paper. For ten or more seconds she couldn't move. She should go... get out of this office. Whatever that—she stared at the note—was about, she didn't want to get dragged into it. The men who had stormed the ER had all been wearing jeans or cargo pants, not dress trousers and certainly not leather loafers. *Just go!*

At the door, she eased it open and checked the administrator's private lobby. Clear. She'd almost made it out of the secretary's office when she heard hurried footfalls in the corridor. Renewed panic roared through her veins.

With nowhere else to go, she ducked under the secretary's desk.

The footfalls moved across the carpeted floor. She heard the sound of Pierce's office door opening. The man was popular tonight. Had the guy who'd written the note forgotten something?

A soft curse came from the general direction of Pierce's office.

Eva hoped SWAT was ready to storm the place. She would hate to survive a bunch of crazed thugs or gangbangers or whatever they were and be murdered by a man wearing dress trousers and black leather shoes.

"Eva!"

For a moment she couldn't breathe.

"Eva!"

Dr. Pierce. She scrambled out from under the desk. "Yes, sir. I'm here."

Fury or outrage—something on that order—colored his face. "The police are here. They'll need your statement."

Thank God. "Is everyone okay? The gunmen have been contained?"

He nodded, then frowned. "I thought you were going to hide in my office."

She shrugged and in that instant something about the expression on his face made her decide to keep what happened in his office to herself. "I heard someone coming. I freaked and hid under the secretary's desk."

"Someone came in here?"

He had to know someone had. He couldn't have missed the disarray in his office or the note on his desk.

She nodded. "I couldn't see what was happening, but I definitely heard footsteps and the door to your office opening and closing."

"You didn't get a look at who it was?"

She shook her head. Was that suspicion she heard in his voice?

When he continued to stare at her without saying more, she offered, "Is everything okay?"

"Yes." He smiled, rearranging his face into the amiable expression he usually wore. "It is now. Come with me. We should get this police business squared away so we can return to the business of healing the sick."

The walk back to the emergency department was the longest of her life. She could feel his tension in every step he took. She wanted to ask him again if everything was okay but she didn't dare stir his suspicions.

Right now all she wanted was for this night to be over.

Chapter Two

Eva hurried up the sidewalk. She glanced over her shoulder repeatedly, checked the street over and over. She hated that her behavior no doubt looked entirely paranoid, but the truth was paranoia had been her constant companion for better than forty-eight hours. Since she received the first message.

Two men had swerved to the curb on her street as she walked home from the market on Saturday afternoon. She might have kept walking except the one hanging out the passenger window called her name.

Eva! Eva Bowman! He's coming for you, la perra. You killed his hermano menor.

The man who'd tried to rape her—the one who'd fractured his skull in that damned bathroom and then died—was the younger brother of one of Chicago's most notorious gang leaders.

Just her luck.

Eva walked faster. She hadn't meant to kill anyone. She'd been fighting for her life. He'd fallen…his death was an accident. An accident that wouldn't have happened had he not been trying to rape her.

The detectives on the scene had tried to make her feel better by telling her that Diego Robles—that was the dead man's name, Diego Robles—and his gang of nearly a dozen thugs had murdered six men and two women on Friday before overtaking the ER where she worked.

Except it hadn't made her feel better. Robles had been nineteen years old. *Nineteen.* He had an older brother, Miguel, who was thirty-five and the leader of the True Disciples, an extremely violent offshoot of the Latin Disciples. The brother had passed along his message to Eva on three occasions without ever leaving a single shred of evidence she could take to the police.

The first warning had come on Saturday afternoon via the two thugs in the car. Another had come when she walked out of the corner coffee shop near her apartment building on Sunday morning. Then, last night, another man had showed up at the ER asking for her. When she'd appeared at the registration desk, he'd waited until no one was looking and leaned forward to whisper for her ears only.

You will die this week.

With that he'd given her a nod and told her to enjoy her night.

She'd reported all three incidents to the police and all they could do was tell her to be careful. No one had touched her or damaged her property. She had no proof of the threats other than her word. But last night when she'd been too afraid to go to her car alone and then too terrified to go to her own apartment, she'd understood she had to do something. She worried the only evidence to back up her fears would come in the form of someone finding her body after it was too late.

Lena had demanded, to no avail, protection from the police for Eva. Kim Levy, her friend and another nurse at the Edge, had urged her to speak to Dr. Pierce. Kim had been in the ER on Friday night. She understood how terrified Eva had every right to be. But Eva couldn't stop thinking about the way Dr. Pierce had looked at her after the strange happenings in his office. She'd decided not to discuss that odd moment with

Kim or anyone else. And she had no desire to discuss her personal dilemma with her boss. Still, Kim being Kim, she had gone to Dr. Pierce and told him what was going on. He had insisted on sending Eva to the Colby Agency. Eva had heard of the Colby Agency. Who hadn't? She'd certainly never expected to need a private investigations firm. Yet, here she was. She had an appointment at two thirty. Five minutes from now.

Almost there. The Magnificent Mile was always busy, even on a Tuesday afternoon with hours to go before the evening rush of commuters headed home. She looked at each face she met…wondering when one of *them* would appear.

She walked faster, pushing against the wind that seemed to want to blow her right back to where she'd parked her car.

No turning back now.

A shiver chilled her skin. It didn't feel very much like spring today. Barely sixty degrees and overcast. Just in case it started to rain again, she'd tucked her umbrella into the beige leather bag she carried. Her pepper spray was in there, too. She carried her life around in one of two bags: a well-used brown one for fall and winter and this tawny beige one her mother had given her for spring and summer. Life was complicated enough without changing the purse she carried more than twice a year. Eva went out of her way to keep life simple. She'd had enough complications her freshman year in college. She'd made a decision all those years ago never to allow those sorts of complications ever again.

Life was better when she stuck to enjoying the simpler pleasures. Like all the gorgeous tulips still in bloom and the trees that had gone from their stark winter limbs to lush and green already.

That was the ticket. Focus on the mundane... the normal.

The deep timbre of male voices was suddenly behind her. Fear crept up her spine like a cluster of spiders and her heart swelled into her throat. Her gait wavered, causing her to nearly stumble. A group of four men moved around and ahead of her. Despite the glaring facts that they paid her absolutely no notice, were dressed in business suits and kept moving at a brisk pace, her heart refused to slide back down into her chest where it belonged. The pepper spray in her bag felt wholly inadequate.

Damn, she was a mess.

It wasn't until she spotted the wide glass front bearing the address of her destination that she was able to breathe easy again. Her hands settled on the door and, despite her best efforts, she hesitated. Calm was the necessary watchword. If she went into this meeting shaken and panicky, she might very well meet with the same reception she'd received from the two Chicago PD detectives working the investigation.

Investigation. There were several aspects of the ongoing investigation. The clash between the True Disciples and another well-known gang with the resulting multiple homicides. The taking of an entire ER hostage. And the deemed justified homicide of Diego Robles. Both detectives, their captain and the DA had told her the events that happened in that bathroom were self-defense, completely justified. She had not intended to kill anyone. She'd only been trying to get away from him. The man's death was an accidental consequence of his actions.

But dead was dead.

Calm. Collected. Not your fault.

Eva squared her shoulders and pushed through the door. A wide, gleaming metal security desk curved around the center of the enormous lobby. Enough greenery to rival a small jungle softened all the glass and glossy metal.

"Afternoon, ma'am," the security guard said as she approached the counter. "You have an appointment?"

"The Colby Agency." She drew her wallet from her bag and produced her driver's license. "Eva Bowman."

The guard checked the computer screen, scanned her license into his system, then handed the license as well as a visitor's badge to her. "The elevators are to your right. Fourteenth floor is where you're headed. Your code for the elevator is on the back of the badge. Just drop the badge off here as you leave, Ms. Bowman."

"Thank you." As she moved toward the bank of elevators, she checked the back of the badge. Eight-two-six-seven. She clipped the badge onto the lapel of her sweater and tapped the call button.

The doors opened to a vacant car. Deep breath. She stepped inside and selected floor fourteen. The keypad warned that a code was required so she entered the necessary digits. When the doors closed she stared at her reflection in the mirrored walls of the elevator interior. She'd taken care to dress professionally. The soft blush color of her pants and sweater set complemented her too-pale skin. Matching leather ballet flats were easy on the feet. Her first month as an ER nurse had taught her to appreciate good shoes made for comfort. She'd swept her blond hair into a loose bun at the nape of her neck and she'd gone easy on the makeup. Just a touch of lip gloss and a swipe of mascara.

Calm. Collected.

The car bumped to a stop and the doors slid open to another lobby. A receptionist looked up from behind an opaque glass desk and smiled. "Good morning. Welcome to the Colby Agency, Ms. Bowman."

The next five or so minutes passed in a blur. After the offer of refreshments, which she declined, another receptionist appeared and escorted her to Victoria Colby-Camp's office, a large, elegant space with a wall of windows that overlooked the city from a prestigious Michigan Avenue address.

Eva had done an internet search on Victoria and her agency, but she hadn't been adequately prepared for the sophisticated woman standing behind the beautiful mahogany desk, the wall of windows a stunning backdrop. She wore her salt-and-pepper hair in a French twist. The turquoise suit fit as if it had been tailored just for her. Probably had been. Though she was no taller than Eva, her presence was commanding. The most surprising part was how incredibly youthful and fit she looked. According to Google, Victoria Colby-Camp was nearing seventy. Eva could only hope she would look that good in another forty years.

"It's a pleasure to meet you, Eva." Victoria smiled. "Please sit. Let's take a moment to get acquainted."

"Thank you." Eva settled into one of the two champagne-colored upholstered chairs in front of Victoria's desk.

"My intern, Jamie, will be joining us shortly," Victoria said. "I've reviewed your file. You're a nurse at the Edge. Dr. Pierce and I serve on Chicago's civic committee together. The Edge is an incredible step toward elevating emergency care to the highest level. We're all very proud and duly impressed by his advances in the field."

Eva nodded. "Dr. Pierce is an amazing man. His methods are changing the landscape of emergency medicine." The Edge was his brainchild. Whether it was a heart attack, a stroke or some sort of physical injury, the Edge was where everyone wanted to end up when an emergency occurred.

"You have family in the city?"

Eva smiled. Her first of the day. "An older

sister, Lena. You may know her. She's an investigative journalist at Channel 7."

Victoria nodded. "I do, indeed. Lena Bowman is a household name in the city of Chicago."

Eva nodded. "She was determined to become one for as long as I can remember."

Victoria tilted her head ever so slightly, her expression turning somber. "I've also had an opportunity to review the Chicago PD's file on what happened Friday night. It's an outright miracle no hostages were killed. You and the others at the Edge handled yourselves extraordinarily well."

Eva nodded in acknowledgment of her kind words. "Since you read the file you must know about Diego Robles's death."

"Captain Cyrus explained what happened. He's very concerned that you've been approached and threatened. Dr. Pierce is immensely concerned as well. Why don't you start at the beginning and tell me what's happening."

As much as Eva had dreaded this part, somehow Victoria made her feel relaxed and comfortable—at least as comfortable as she could be under the circumstances. Eva started with what the second man who came into the bathroom on Friday night said to her. She moved on to the ones who'd shouted at her on the street on Saturday, the confrontation on Sunday, the visit at the ER last night and then to the carful of thugs who had followed her to the parking garage three blocks from here. Thankfully, they hadn't yelled more threats at her…they'd only watched her. Their hateful eyes on her had been equally threatening.

Victoria studied Eva for a moment after she finished recounting the events of the past three days. "I have full confidence the police are watching Robles's men, but they can't watch every move each of his hundreds of followers make—not with the budget cuts they've suffered recently. You haven't been assigned a protection detail for the same reason. Until a law is broken, the police can't afford to shift the resources."

"I might be dead by then." Eva hated to say the words aloud but they were true.

"Which is why we're here. We can fill that void." Victoria folded her hands atop her desk. "Since Dr. Pierce and I are well acquainted, he asked that I assign the very best to your security and he insisted that I send the bill to him."

"What?" Eva shook her head. She couldn't have heard correctly. "I'm prepared to pay for the services I need."

Victoria held up a hand. "I'm certain you are, Eva. But Dr. Pierce feels responsible. He would like to handle this and, frankly, he can easily afford to do so. Trust me, you should take him up on his generous offer."

Eva wanted to argue, but Victoria was right. She had scratched together the retainer but she would be hard-pressed to come up with more than a week's worth of the required fees. She wanted to be upset that Dr. Pierce had been brought into the financial aspect of this arrangement but she supposed it was the right thing to do. *I know what you did.* The note someone had left on his desk blotter flickered across her mind. She had no idea what the message meant or who left it. She had wanted to ask Dr. Pierce but with all that had happened that night and then the threats, she'd forgotten. In truth, she didn't feel comfortable discussing it with him after his reaction that night. She wasn't worried that he somehow felt she was involved or aware of who went into his office, but she couldn't quite dispel the idea that he'd looked at her with doubt for just a moment.

"I suppose I can do that."

Maybe when this business with Robles was behind her she would come clean and tell Dr. Pierce she'd lied about being in his office.

God, Eva, you're such an idiot. It would have been so much easier if she'd told the truth in the first place, but it had felt so awkward in that instant. As badly as she felt about that decision, she had far more serious issues with which to deal at present.

"Good." Victoria picked up a manila folder on her desk and opened it. "When I assign one of my people to a case, I do all within my power to ensure I'm covering every possible need a client might have."

The door opened and a woman walked in. Blond hair, blue eyes. She was tall and thin. Very young. High school, maybe a college freshman. As young as she was, she held herself in a regal manner that reminded Eva of Victoria.

"I apologize for the delay." The girl smiled first at Victoria then at Eva. "I'm Jamie Colby." She offered her hand to Eva.

Eva shook Jamie's hand, noting the firm confidence in her grip.

"Eva, this is my granddaughter," Victoria said, pride brimming in her tone. "She's a sophomore at the University of Chicago and my intern two days a week."

"You look so young," Eva blurted before she could stop herself, "to have accomplished so much."

"Jamie is quite special," Victoria agreed.

Jamie smiled. "I took freshman classes my senior year of high school. It's not so unusual that I'm eighteen and a sophomore and certainly not special."

Her humility was refreshing. Eva said, "I'm certain your parents are very pleased."

"They certainly are." Victoria turned to Jamie. "All is in order?"

"It is," Jamie assured her.

"As I was saying—" Victoria turned to Eva "—I take great pride in assigning the best person for the job. Since your bodyguard—"

"Bodyguard?" Eva expected an investigator to help with the Miguel Robles situation, not a bodyguard.

Victoria and Jamie shared a look before Victoria's gaze settled on Eva once more. "We need to take this situation very seriously, Eva. Frankly, I'm surprised you're not already dead."

Eva's breath caught. She put her hand over her mouth too late to catch the sound.

"Ms. Bowman," Jamie said, turning in her chair to face Eva, "I've done extensive research on the True Disciples. Miguel Robles raised his younger brother since their parents were murdered fifteen years ago. He thought of Diego as more of a son than a brother.

Typically when crossed, Miguel wields vengeance far more quickly and concisely. The idea that you're alive three days later tells us that he is planning to make some sort of example out of you. He wants you to know it's coming. He wants to watch your fear build. He wants a large audience and rumor on the street is that all eyes are on you right now."

Eva blinked repeatedly to hold back the rush of tears. "Wait, this is crazy. I didn't mean to kill his brother. He attacked me... I..."

When Eva's voice failed her, Victoria said, "I'm afraid it only gets worse. Chicago PD has a unit called Gang Intelligence. Though they cannot provide any measure of security for you, they are watching. If you want my honest opinion, they're hoping Robles will come after you. If they can catch Miguel Robles in the act of trying to harm you, they can bring down a man who has slipped through their fingers repeatedly over the past two decades."

Oh God. "I think I see the whole picture now." Eve swallowed at the lump still lodged in her throat. "I'm bait. The police won't protect me—not because of budget cuts—but because they want to get this guy."

"In all fairness," Victoria reminded her,

"no law has been broken—more or less tying their hands. At this time all anyone has are rumors and suspicions, and resources are stretched too thin already. I fully believe the police are doing all they legally can."

Jamie placed a warm hand over Eva's ice-cold one. "But we can take up that slack."

"Dr. Pierce has granted us full access to his facility," Victoria explained. "We'd like to provide around-the-clock protection until this situation is neutralized."

Round-the-clock? "Is that really necessary?" The moment the words left her lips she felt foolish for having said them.

Eva hadn't expected this insanity to consume her life. Her sister had told her it was bad. She'd spent the past two nights with Eva. If all that Victoria said was true, Lena being close put her in danger as well. Eva suddenly felt immensely grateful that Lena's boss had called about a hot-button issue in DC and wanted her there ASAP. Lena had nearly refused to go but Eva had promised she would be fine with the Colby Agency taking care of her. After considerable persuasion, her sister had reluctantly accepted the assignment. Eva now completely understood how important it was to keep Lena as far from this as possible...and to end this as quickly as possible.

"Okay," Eva heard herself say. "When do I meet this bodyguard?"

"As Victoria explained," Jamie cut in, "we take every precaution when making the selection. Your situation requires extensive training. The man we've chosen spent eight years in the military, six in the Army's Special Forces. He is an expert in all manner of defense and protection. His extensive emergency medical training will allow a smooth transition into your workplace. He's the perfect choice."

Victoria nodded her agreement. "You couldn't be in better hands."

Eva's head was still spinning. She could do this. It was necessary. Her boss understood. Lena would come unglued if Eva even thought of backing out of hiring the Colby Agency. This was the right step. *Just do this.* "All right. I'm ready to do whatever I have to."

"Before we ask him in," Victoria began.

Eva instinctively understood that something bad was coming.

"We've been made aware that there may be a stumbling block of sorts. Under normal circumstances," Victoria went on, "I never make assignments when there are personal connections. Emotions can often get in the way."

Eva shook her head. "I'm sorry. This is my first time here and I'm fairly confident I don't know anyone at your agency."

"Todd Christian."

Eva's head turned so quickly toward the woman seated next to her that her neck almost snapped. "Todd Christian?"

Impossible. Even as the word filtered through her, Eva comprehended it was not. Todd had gone straight from college into the military. She'd heard at some point later that he was in some sort of special something but she couldn't remember what. She had spent the past nine years blocking every single thing about him from her brain. Todd Christian no longer existed as far as Eva was concerned. She had worked extremely hard to make that happen.

Jamie nodded. "He is the perfect choice."

Eva shook her head. "No. Absolutely not." She could not—would not—spend one minute much less 24/7 with him. No damned way.

Another of those looks passed between Victoria and her granddaughter.

"Todd thought you might feel that way," Victoria offered. "Eva, let me just say that I've been doing this for a very long time."

"A seriously long time," Jamie echoed.

"I do not make a suggestion such as this

lightly," Victoria continued. "I ask that you put your personal feelings aside for a moment before you request an alternate choice. Toward that end, Todd has asked if he might speak with you privately before you make your final decision."

"He's here?" Stupid question. He worked here. Of course he would be somewhere on the floor. Eva felt the heat rise in her face and then, just as suddenly, the color drain away, leaving her as weak as a kitten. How could she face him? He was the last person on Earth she wanted to hear about her personal issues.

"With your permission, Jamie and I will wait in my private lobby while the two of you talk for a moment."

"There must be someone else." Eva shook her head again. This would never do. "You mentioned an alternate choice."

Victoria set her hands palms down on her desk and stood. "I pride myself in hiring only the best, Eva. Of course, there are others, but no one who would fit as seamlessly into your world. To make sure you are protected in such a way that the enemy will not simply lay low until that protection ceases, we must ensure they are taken by surprise. The last thing we want is for Robles to step back and wait out your resources. This is the only way to guarantee the outcome you desire in the quickest manner."

As crazy as it sounded, Eva had to admit that she could see her point. But could she do this? Could she allow *him* back into her life? Uncertainty and a new kind of fear coiled inside her like a snake ready to strike.

"I'll speak to him." Eva took a big breath. "I can at least do that."

Victoria nodded. "Excellent."

Jamie patted Eva on the hand and stood. "We'll give you a few moments, but we'll be right outside."

Eva tried to smile but her lips wouldn't make the transition.

When the door closed behind the two women, Eva stood and smoothed a wrinkle out of her sweater hem. Slow, deep breaths.

The door opened and she turned to face the man who had shattered her heart when she was barely old enough to understand what love was. He'd been a senior, she a freshman. She'd never lived anywhere but at home with her parents and sister until she moved into that college dormitory. Lena had gone to Europe for a year of studies abroad. And Eva had fallen madly, deeply in love with the man who taught her what a real orgasm felt like.

She might have been able to say the thirty-two-year-old man who walked into the room and closed the door behind him hadn't changed one bit except that would be utterly and completely wrong. He seemed taller somehow, his shoulders even broader. Her gaze moved down his torso, over the ridges hidden behind the crisp blue oxford she knew all too well. The long sleeves ended at his wrists where the wide hands and blunt-tipped fingers that had touched her as if she was all that mattered in this world to him didn't look as smooth as they once had. Long legs were camouflaged by navy trousers tailored to mold perfectly to the powerful muscles beneath. She blinked and shifted her gaze to the handsome face she'd dreamed of every night for years even after he left her. His face looked the slightest bit leaner, more angular, and there was a small scar on his right cheek. His lips…his pale, pale blue eyes— She shifted her gaze from his face. His brown hair was still more blond than brown and in need of a trim. So many little things had changed and yet her body reacted to his mere presence as if absolutely nothing were different. Fire licked a path along every nerve ending.

His lips—the ones that had instructed her in the true art of kissing—slid into a smile. "Eva… It's good to see you."

The hesitation after he said her name told her he was savoring it. Something else she'd yearned for night and day. The sound of his voice, the pull of every syllable he uttered. Chill bumps rose on her skin. The smile…the sound of his voice, his presence in the room even after all these years had the ability to make her nervous. Made her ache for things she couldn't name.

Eva commanded the butterflies that had come to life in her stomach to go away. She stared directly into those gorgeous eyes of his. "Is it true, what they say? That you can protect me better than anyone else employed at the Colby Agency?"

"You have my word."

Those four little words—damn him—sent another shiver racing over her too-hot skin. "I'll need more than your word, Christian." She refused to call him Todd. She could not. "You see, I learned long ago that your word is of little value."

"I hurt you, Eva," he confessed. "You haven't forgiven me and maybe I don't deserve your forgiveness, but if you'll trust me now I swear on my life that I will take care of this for you. Let me do that. Please."

The idea that she could spend the next few days making him damned miserable held some appeal. "Fine. I trust *your boss*. She says you're the man for the job. We'll see about that."

"Good."

She picked up her bag and slung it over her shoulder. "Make sure you remember that once we walk out of this building *I* am the boss."

He nodded his agreement, and just like that she jumped right out of the frying pan and into the fire.

Chapter Three

Eva didn't want him close. She'd insisted on driving separately to her building. He hadn't liked it but she'd given him no choice. He'd stayed right on her bumper on the drive from the agency to her address. Rather than warn him about the parking situation, she'd driven into the covered area for tenants and he'd had to fend for himself on the street. When he'd finally found a spot, he'd had to hurry to catch up to her before she reached the building.

Like it or not, that would not happen again. Next time they would be in the same vehicle *together*.

At the front entrance she entered the code for the door and walked in, letting go of the door as she did. The damned thing almost closed before Todd caught it. She didn't look back, obviously unconcerned as to whether he made it inside.

He hadn't really expected her to forgive him—not even after nearly ten years. Not ever, most likely. Under the circumstances he was hoping for some sort of cordiality or at least a temporary truce.

Inside, rather than going for the elevator, she headed to the door marked with the stairwell logo. No problem. He hefted his duffel onto one shoulder and followed her. His time in the service had taught him not to take his physical condition for granted. He stayed in the same shape he had when he'd been in active duty.

The climb to the third floor, however, gave him far too much time to focus on the sway of her hips. Someone else stayed in shape, he decided. He remembered her soft curves a little too well. Time had been good to her. She still looked like the nineteen-year-old he'd first met in the university library. He'd tried so damned hard to focus on the book he'd been reading for an English paper, only he couldn't stop looking at her over the top of the page. She had the blondest hair, still did. Every sweet hair on her gorgeous body was naturally blond. Her skin was the creamiest white, like porcelain. And those eyes, so green. When she smiled or got angry they shimmered like emeralds under a waterfall.

She exited the stairwell on the third floor, again without looking back or saying a word to him. He followed. This was another part they had to get straight. He went through any door first. She stayed close and behind him, preferably.

He imagined the real trouble was going to be in getting her to cooperate when he explained that she might be the boss but he was in charge.

At the door to her apartment he stepped in front of her. "I go in first." He held out his hand.

She dropped the key into his palm and stepped back. He unlocked the door and moved inside. He'd looked at the floor plans for her building. She had a one-bedroom. The entry door opened into a small hall. The living and dining space along with the kitchen were an L-shape, and then another tiny hall with doors to a linen closet, the bedroom and the bath. No balcony, but she did have two large windows. He motioned for her to come inside, but she didn't. She stared at the door across the hall.

"Something wrong?"

She shook her head. "Guess not." She gestured to the door she'd been staring at. "I thought my neighbor was going out of town." With a shrug she turned to her own door and stepped inside.

Todd closed and locked it. "Stay put until I have a look around."

She rolled her eyes and folded her arms over her chest.

The large window overlooking the street allowed plenty of light into the room. He was surprised there were no blinds or curtains. The Eva he had known before had been very shy and private. Another of those things that had attracted him. He was glad to see an upholstered sofa rather than leather since it would serve as his bed. A small cocktail table stood in front of the sofa and a side table sat between two comfortable-looking chairs. The upholstery and the throw pillows were soft, muted shades of blues and greens and yellows. A rug in the center of the room was scattered with two larger pillows. Didn't take much to imagine her on the floor curled up with a good book. Back in college she'd enjoyed reading romance novels when she wasn't studying. He'd often teased her about her secret hobby.

The kitchen was tiny with an even tinier dining area. Updated three-piece bath with lots of that subway tile people went gaga over. Big mirrors that made the space look a tad larger and more of those little bursts of color that adorned the main living space. He opened the door to the bedroom and the scent of her assaulted him and made him weak. The large window in this intimate space was covered with thick curtains, ensuring the room was dark. He flipped on a light, checked the closet that overflowed with clothes and shoes and then turned to go. The unmade bed and the nightshirt tossed onto the tousled covers made him hesitate.

Selfishly, he experienced a sense of satisfaction at the untouched second pillow on the bed. He scanned the walls and other surfaces for photos or signs of a boyfriend. The only photographs were of her and her sister, Lena, and their parents. Their father had died the year before Eva started college. She had still been struggling with the loss when they were together.

"Are you finished yet?"

He pivoted toward her voice, surprised she'd gotten as far as the door without him noticing. *Distraction is dangerous*. He knew better. "The apartment is clear."

"I noticed." She executed an about-face and stormed away.

Todd heaved a disgusted breath and plowed his hand through his hair. This might not be as easy as he'd thought. He had foolishly hoped they might be able to make amends. That maybe he and Eva could be friends now that he was back in Chicago. Guess not.

He exited the bedroom and took the few short steps to the kitchen. This place was considerably smaller than it looked when he reviewed the building's floor plan. Spending a lot of time here with her would prove less than comfortable. She opened cabinet door after cabinet door, then rummaged in the refrigerator, obviously looking for something to eat.

"We could have dinner delivered," he suggested.

She looked at him over the fridge door. "Yogurt and crackers are fine with me."

He gritted his teeth and restrained any response for a moment. Her plan was obvious—make him as miserable as possible. No problem. He deserved it. "Sounds awesome."

She blinked but not fast enough to cover her surprise. A carton of yogurt and an apple in hand, she left the fridge, grabbed a box of crackers from a cabinet and carried her haul to the counter.

He tossed his duffel on the sofa and watched

as she carefully sliced her apple and arranged it on a plate, then added a handful of small crackers. With yogurt spooned into the center, she sprinkled a few walnuts on top. Spoon and plate in hand, she carried both to the made-for-two dining table. She poured herself a glass of water from the pitcher in the fridge, grabbed a napkin and then took a seat.

Todd ignored her indifference and made himself at home. He grabbed a plate, rummaged for a butter knife, found peanut butter and proceeded to slather it onto as many of the small crackers as the plate would hold. He added an apple, not bothering to slice it, poured a glass of water and then joined her at the small table.

"Looks like you predicted Lena's future correctly." He stuffed a cracker into his mouth, hoping the protein in the peanut butter would satisfy him. He was starving.

Eva licked the yogurt from her spoon. He stared at his plate, then went for the apple. Anything to avoid watching her tongue slide around on that spoon.

"Channel 7 loves her. The viewers love her." Eva nibbled on a cracker. "I'm really proud of her."

Todd knocked back a long swallow of water before placing his glass back on the table.

"You haven't done so bad yourself. Pierce raved about you to Victoria."

"I'm happy." She reached for an apple slice.

She didn't ask about his career or whether he was happy or if his brother Kevin was okay. The only part that surprised him was Kevin. His brother had been just a toddler when their father abandoned them. Their mother had died a few months earlier and there was no known extended family. Kevin had been adopted quickly, but Todd hadn't been so lucky. He'd spent the next twelve years of his life in foster homes. It wasn't until college that his little brother found him. They'd been damned close since. Eva was the only woman he'd ever taken to Christmas dinner with Kevin. He had loved her. She always asked about Kevin after that…at least until Todd left. Then again, he couldn't really hold that against her since he hadn't exactly been around for her when her mother died. He pushed the sensitive memory away.

The rest of the not-so-yummy and definitely not-filling meal was consumed without conversation. She rinsed her plate and placed it in the dishwasher. He pushed in his chair and followed her lead with the cleanup. "If only we had dessert."

She didn't smile. Instead she walked to the

cabinets, put the crackers away and withdrew a tub of cake frosting. She shoved it at him. "Chocolate. Enjoy."

Really? He put the frosting back in the cabinet and joined her in the living room. Since she obviously had no desire to catch up, he might as well move on to business. "How much do you know about the True Disciples?"

She curled up in one of the two chairs and started channel surfing with the sound muted. "Only what the police told me."

He took the other seat. Since she kept the volume off he viewed that as an invitation to talk. "Miguel Robles's father, Jorge, immigrated to Chicago in the '80s. He became deeply involved in the Latin Disciples. About fifteen years ago, there was a falling-out between Jorge and the leader of the Latin Disciples. Jorge walked away, starting his own band of merry men. Five years later, Jorge found himself facing cancer, so he started the transition of power to Miguel. A decade from now Miguel, since he has no children of his own, would likely have been doing the same with Diego."

With her sister's channel on the screen, Eva set the remote aside and turned her attention to Todd. "He sees me as the person who not only stole his younger brother's life but also as the person who turned his entire future upside down."

The situation was far graver than she understood. "Avenging Diego's death is a matter of honor, Eva. Whatever else happens, he has no choice but to kill you or lose face. Personally, I don't understand why the police didn't take you into protective custody."

She glared at him as if he'd offended her. "Your boss said there aren't enough resources to go around."

Victoria was right about that part, but the sheer enormity of the situation should have prompted a stronger reaction. Not that he was suggesting the police didn't want to stop Miguel, but sometimes he wondered if their priorities were in order.

"That's true," he admitted. "But some cases fall outside the parameters of the norm. Those cases should be evaluated differently. Yours, in my humble opinion, is one of those cases."

She laughed. "You've never been humble in your life." With that announcement, she pushed up from her chair and walked to the window.

Maybe there was a time when her pronouncement was true, but not anymore. He hesitated only a moment before joining her. On the street below the traffic was heavy. The neighborhood was a nice one. Towering, mature trees lined the street. Much-desired shopping and restaurants were only a few blocks away. He'd driven past her building more than once since his return to Chicago last year. Mentioning that too-telling fact would hardly be a good thing, he decided.

"I'm sure you're aware that the police see you as their first real opportunity to get this guy."

She nodded. "Your boss mentioned it."

"I can understand how much they want him and the idea that using you as bait somehow serves the greater good, but I'm not them. My job is to protect you at all costs."

She glanced at him, the worry in her eyes tugging at his gut.

"So let's not make you an easy target by standing in front of this window." He touched her arm. She stiffened but he curled his fingers around the soft limb anyway and gently tugged her back to the pair of chairs they had deserted.

Rather than sit down, she stared up at him. She searched his eyes, worry clouding hers. "Do you really believe you can stop him?" She licked her lips, drawing his attention there. He remembered her taste as vividly as if he'd only just kissed her. "That all by yourself," she said, dragging him from the forbidden memory, "you can somehow do what the police haven't been able to do in what? A decade?"

No matter the seriousness of her question, this close he almost smiled at the small sprinkling of freckles on her nose and cheeks. She had hated those tiny freckles and he had loved them. This close he noticed there was a line or two on her gorgeous face that hadn't been there before, but those fine lines only added to her beauty. He wanted her to trust him. He desperately wanted her to believe in him again. Whatever else she thought of him, he would never lie to her. He hadn't lied all those years ago and he wasn't about to start now.

"First, I don't operate by the same rules as the police. Giving them grace, their hands are tied to some degree by the very laws they've sworn to uphold. Second, I can't promise I'll be able to stop Robles, but I can promise that I'll die trying."

EVA PULLED FREE of his touch and turned away from him. She couldn't bear the way he looked at her...as if he truly cared. Of course he probably possessed some basic human compassion for her as a person but otherwise she was nothing more than an assignment and maybe a potential opportunity for sexual release. Not that finding willing women would be an issue for him—it hadn't been a decade ago and it certainly wouldn't be now. He was still incredibly handsome and far too charming.

She closed her eyes. *So not fair, Eva.* She didn't know the man standing in her apartment right now. She knew the college guy he used to be. The super hot guy who seemed to show up in the library every Tuesday and Thursday evening just like she had. The guy with the beautiful lean, muscled body and scruffy, thick hair that made her want to twine her fingers in it while she traced every line and ridge of his healthy male body with her other hand. The guy who stole her heart and ruined her for anyone else.

Not once in ten years had she been kissed the way Todd Christian kissed her. Not a single time in the last decade had another man—not that there had been very many—made love to her the way Todd Christian had.

Eva hugged her arms around herself. What kind of fool permitted *that* guy back into her life?

A desperate one.

A *splat, splat, splat* echoed in the room. The window rattled in its frame. Eva instinctively backed up, her body bumping into his. Rivulets of red rained down from a cloud of red in the center of the window.

Todd pulled her behind the chairs. "Stay down while I have a look."

He moved across the room and took a position next to the window, out of sight from whoever was out there firing something at her window. Eva peeked around the chair and studied the damage to the window. It didn't appear broken or cracked. The splats looked like the ones made by a paintball gun.

Was this just another warning from the man who wanted his revenge?

"We need something to cover this window."

Todd was suddenly standing over her, holding out his hand. She ignored it and stood. "I have extra sheets in the linen closet."

He nodded. "You round those up while I give Detective Marsh an update."

"Are you working with the police?" She didn't know why she was surprised. The Colby Agency was a prominent firm. Her internet research had indicated that Victoria was known and respected by everyone who was anyone in Chicago. She'd been voted woman of the year more than once.

"Just keeping them up to speed on what's

going on. If I play nice, hopefully they'll do the same for me."

She nodded. Made sense. While he spoke to the detective she went to the bathroom. She'd tried really hard the past few days to stay strong. To keep it together. The first day, Saturday, hadn't been so bad. Her sister had kept her mind off the horror of the previous night until Eva went unconscious from sheer exhaustion.

In the bathroom, she closed the door and sagged against it. But then the threats had begun. Eva was so thankful when Lena was sent out of town. No matter that her sister had wanted to stay and had insisted that she dove into the fray of danger every time she walked onto a hot news scene, this was different. Eva was the target. She felt certain this Miguel Robles would like nothing better than to use her sister to hurt her. At least she didn't have to worry so much about that part right now. Lena would be in Washington, DC, for several days.

With her sister safely out of reach, Eva could focus on keeping herself alive.

The memory of her neighbor's door nagged at her. Mrs. Cackowski had mentioned going to New York to visit her daughter. The plan was she would leave today and spend the upcoming Mother's Day weekend with her daughter and her family. She would fly back next Tuesday. Mrs. Cackowski said flying on Tuesdays was cheaper. Eva wasn't entirely sure that was true but the idea appeared to make the older lady happy.

The trouble was, the No Solicitors magnet was not on her door. Mrs. Cackowski and Eva had a routine. Whenever her neighbor was away from home, whether for the day or for a week, she put the magnet on her door. When she returned, it was removed. This way, even if Eva missed talking to her she knew to keep an eye on the elderly woman's apartment. She usually left a key with Eva so she could water her plants if it was an extended vacation, but not this time.

Maybe her neighbor's flight had been changed at the last minute. If Mrs. Cackowski would break down and get a cell phone, Eva could call and check with her. She should probably call the property manager and tell him about the red paint—or whatever it was—all over her window. The two windows in her apartment didn't open so it wasn't like she could clean it up herself. Since she faced the street her neighbors wouldn't be happy about the unsightly mess.

A knock on the door had her jumping away from it. "You okay in there?"

Eva put her hand to her throat. "Fine. I just need a moment."

She went to the sink and turned on the water. How was she supposed to deal with all this? Her actions had caused a man's death. Shouldn't she feel something besides empty and cold about it by now? Last night a patient had required a psychological consult. After the doctor had assessed the patient, Eva had spoken to the psychiatrist briefly about what happened to her. He'd warned that she was in the shock and denial phase right now. In time the reality would hit and she might fall apart. *Start counseling now*, he'd warned.

Like every other nurse and doctor she knew, the last person she wanted to spend time fixing was herself. It was far easier to take care of everyone else's problems. Funny how she'd worked so hard and long to keep her life simple. Work, eat, sleep and repeat. Once in a great while she bothered with dating.

How had her simple existence turned so suddenly complicated?

Maybe the shrink had been right about the shock and denial. She had pretty much been attempting to pretend Friday night never happened. She might have been successful if not for the continued threats.

After splashing some water on her face, she reached for the hand towel and dabbed her skin dry. At this point she didn't know if she had enough time left to reach the reality phase.

She could be dead before then.

Chapter Four

Wednesday, May 9, 8:15 a.m.

Eva scarcely slept at all. Between worrying about what the gang leader Miguel Robles might do next and the idea that Todd Christian was on her sofa, how could she hope to sleep? At some point after two this morning, she'd finally drifted to sleep only to dream about being chased by killers. She'd jerked awake in a cold sweat to the sound of the shower.

For the next several minutes she'd battled with her errant mind and its inability to control the wellspring of images involving Todd Christian naked in her shower. When he'd finished and she was certain he'd moved to the kitchen, she reluctantly headed to the bathroom. With the water as hot as she could bear it, she still couldn't wash away the scent of him…it clung to the tile walls, to the bar of homemade soap a friend had given her, insisting that no bodywash on the planet could compete. Despite rinsing the soap thoroughly, simply smoothing the bar over her skin aroused her. Shivers tumbled over her skin with every slow stroke. Her nipples hardened with the sweet ache of need and she once again found herself fighting to keep memories of their lovemaking at bay. How could those memories still be so vivid? So intoxicating?

Todd Christian was like an addictive drug. And like the wrong kind of drug, he was bad for her.

By the time she turned off the water she felt ready to explode with tension. Taking her time, she dried her skin and then her hair. By the time she finished, she had gone from the edge of orgasm to teeth-grinding frustration.

This arrangement was not going to work. No way, no how.

Shoulders squared, purple Wednesday scrubs and her most comfortable nursing clogs on, she walked into the kitchen to tell the bane of her existence he had to sleep somewhere else. She could not have him in her apartment like this. There had to be some other arrangement. Might as well get it over with now and salvage what little sanity she had left. The sooner, the better.

"Good morning." He smiled and saluted her with his coffee mug. "I scrambled a few eggs and popped in some toast while you were showering. Hope you don't mind."

If the scent of the freshly made toast and the coffee hadn't distracted her, she might have been able to hang on to her determination. Instead, her need for fuel took over and she decided she would tell him this wasn't going to work as soon as she ate. Why let the food get cold? The least she could do was be civil. If she let her frustration show she would only look immature. She would die before she allowed him to see how easily he could still get to her.

"Morning." She poured a cup of coffee and reached for a slice of toast.

The sheets they'd tacked up over the living room window last night blocked the morning light she usually enjoyed. The lack of natural light was a stark reminder that her life was a mess. She had killed a man.

She sagged against the counter. Didn't matter that she hadn't meant to kill him; he was dead just the same. Nineteen years old. A damn kid.

"Don't go there, Eva."

She blinked, his voice pulling her from the troubling thoughts. "I… I was just thinking about work."

He shook his head. "You were thinking about what happened in that bathroom on Friday night. The pain was written all over your face."

How the hell could he still read her so well all these years later? It wasn't fair. Just another reason he had to go. Today. She absolutely could not allow him back into her life. She'd thought she could handle this situation, but she couldn't. It was impossible. Unrealistic.

"You don't know me anymore, Todd." She set her cup aside and grabbed one of the two plates he'd placed on the counter. She raked a few eggs into the plate and snagged a fork. "I'm not the same naive young girl I was ten years ago."

He stared at her with that intensity she knew all too well. "No, you definitely are not."

She bit back the urge to demand what he meant by his statement.

He pushed off the counter on the opposite side of the island and reached for the remaining plate. She told herself not to watch every damned move he made but somehow she couldn't stop herself. It was like driving past an accident—no amount of willpower would prevent her from looking. His fingers wrapped around the fork and he lifted the eggs to his mouth. His lips closed over the silver tines. Her mouth watered and she forced her attention back to her own fork. She poked a bite of eggs and stuffed them into her mouth. Butter, eggs, cheese and pepper combined into an incredible burst of flavor on her tongue. Simple but so tasty. Most mornings she grabbed a cup of yogurt or a breakfast bar and devoured it on the way to work. A groan of utter satisfaction slipped past her lips.

"Thank you." He grinned. "You still love cheesy scrambled eggs."

The bite of toast she'd taken was suddenly like cardboard on her tongue. How could she have forgotten how he made eggs with cheese and toast for her every time she stayed over at his place? More important, how could he remember something as mundane as eggs and cheese?

She finished off her coffee and glanced at her watch. "I should go."

Before he could say something else she didn't want to hear, she disappeared into the bathroom, which also prevented her from having to look at him. She brushed her teeth and put her hair up in a clip, then stared at her reflection. It didn't take a shrink to narrow down the issue in front of her right now. Todd was the only man she'd ever loved—her first love. He'd taught her how to appreciate her body and to appreciate sex. How to fall completely in love with him. He'd allowed her to believe that what they had was never going to end.

Only it had.

She might have been able to forgive him, to put it behind her and never look back, except that she hadn't been able to fall in love again. No one had been able to lure her down that path or even near it. No matter that an entire decade had passed, she could not feel for anyone else what she had felt for Todd Christian.

Staring at her reflection, Eva realized the one thing that really mattered in all this: staying alive. All this lamenting over how he left her and ruined her for any other man was ridiculous. A man was dead. She had killed him. And now his older brother wanted vengeance. Whining and complaining about the apparent best man to protect her until the situation was sorted out was ridiculous. Worse, it was childish and petulant. She was a grown damn woman. A nurse, for God's sake.

It was time she starting acting like a ma-

ture woman rather than a heartbroken college girl. And she would be damned if she
would let him see just how much power he
still held over her.

Summoning the courage that allowed her
to work in one of the region's most demanding ERs, she walked out of the bathroom and
grabbed her bag. "I'll see you at the hospital."

He dried his hands on the rooster-embel-
lished hand towel she'd thought matched so
well with the simple decorating scheme in
her kitchen—the kitchen he had cleaned up
after preparing breakfast. She ignored the
gesture. What else was he going to do while
he waited for her? The whole breakfast and
cleanup thing was probably just his way of
killing time.

"We should ride together, Eva. It's far
more—"

"Then I guess you'll be riding with me."
She headed for the door. He was not going
to be in charge of every aspect of her existence until this was over. It was bad enough
he'd invaded her home and her dreams. She
wasn't giving him any more power.

She walked out the door and waited until
he'd done the same. Once the door was locked
she turned to head for the stairwell but hesitated. Still nothing on Mrs. Cackowski's door.

She'd forgotten to call and ask the property manager if he'd spoken to her. *You're a bad neighbor, Eva.*

"Give me a minute," she muttered to her shadow. Without further explanation she banged on her neighbor's door loud enough to wake the dead. No answer. No TV sounds. Eva knocked again. An entire minute passed with no answer.

"I can open the door if you'd like."

She glared at him. "You're offering to break into my neighbor's apartment?"

He shrugged those broad, broad shoulders and smiled. "If you bang any harder you're going to break the door down anyway. Trust me, my way is a lot less messy."

"I can call the property manager." She frowned. "I should have done that already."

"Why waste the time? I'll only be a couple of seconds."

For three seconds she thought about telling him to screw off, but then she thought of the men who had followed her and made all those threats—the men who had killed no telling how many people already. What if Mrs. Cackowski was in there bleeding to death? "Okay. Fine. Open the door."

He stepped toward the door in question,

forcing her to back away. Another thought occurred to her. "This can't be legal."

That grin appeared on his lips once more. "Not in any way, shape or form."

Good grief. She knew this. No more pretending. Her cognitive abilities were officially compromised. "Then why are you doing it?"

"Because you asked me to."

"Just stop!" She could not think straight with him around. Damn it! She should just go to work and hope she didn't kill any patients.

"Too late." He gave the door a push and it swung inward.

For a moment Eva couldn't move. She felt frozen to the spot. This felt wrong. No, that wasn't true. Mrs. Cackowski's absence without putting out the damned magnetic sign was wrong.

"Would you like me to go in and check on her?"

His voice snapped Eva into action. "No. I'll do it." She glanced first right then left. Thank God none of her other neighbors were in the hall to see what they were doing.

Eva took a breath and crossed the threshold. Why not add the entering to the breaking? "Mrs. Cackowski, are you home?"

The living room was tidy as always. Mrs. Cackowski had told her how when she moved in years ago she had brought with her the salmon-colored sofa her husband had purchased for their tenth anniversary some forty years back. Three hand crocheted dollies lined the camelbacked sofa. The upholstered chair that swiveled and rocked in which her neighbor spent her days, the coffee table where she served tea every time Eva visited, all looked exactly as it should.

Except there was no Mrs. Cackowski. No sign of a struggle or any other untoward activity. She called her neighbor's name again. Still no answer.

Todd abruptly moved past her and checked the kitchen. Irritation nudged Eva. "Excuse me. This is my neighbor's home. What happened to me having a look around while you wait at the door?"

He shot her a wink. "I've never been a patient man."

Well, now, that was the truth...except when it came to making love. His ability to hold out, to restrain his own needs for hers, had seemed boundless.

No more thinking about sex, Eva. She followed him to the bedroom. No Mrs. Cackowski. Bed was made. He reached for the closet door. "What are you doing?"

He shrugged. "We've come this far."

She stormed up to the door. "I'm certain Mrs. Cackowski would be more comfortable with me checking her closet."

He held up his hands and backed away. "Whatever you say. This time," he warned.

She glared at him, then opened the door. The closet was as neat and undisturbed as the rest of the apartment. Her suitcase sat on the floor of the closet next to a neatly arranged row of practical shoes. Had she bought a new suitcase? Eva shook her head. Maybe the trip had been cancelled. Maybe her neighbor was merely at an appointment. Paranoia was obviously taking full control.

Eva slammed the door. "Let's just go before we get caught."

She walked back to the living room. Todd hurried around her and out the front door before she realized he was right behind her. She glanced back at her neighbor's favorite chair once more. Maybe the elderly woman's age was finally catching up to her and she'd simply forgotten to tell Eva her plans had changed. She turned the thumb lock on the knob. She couldn't lock the deadbolt without the key but at least she could secure the door.

Eva had the number for Mrs. Cackowski's daughter—maybe she'd give her a call today just to be sure. This Robles business was making her second-guess everything.

Once the door was locked again, they left. Todd entered the stairwell ahead of her, then gave her the all clear. Eva reminded herself that he was doing his job. The situation was serious so she should let him. Tamping down her frustration for now, she followed her bodyguard down the stairs and through the lobby.

As they exited the building the burst of fresh air helped her mood a little. The sweet smell of the azaleas lining the sidewalk lifted her spirits. She could make this a better day. All she had to do was keep the proper mindset. Focus on her work. Maybe tonight she'd go to the gym and run a few miles on the treadmill. Running always did amazing things for her outlook. She and her sister participated in a couple of 5k runs every year in memory of their mother and in support of breast cancer research.

Todd suddenly stopped. His arm went out, blocking Eva's path. "Stay behind me and call 911."

When she would have asked why, her gaze settled on her car. The windshield and the two windows she could see had been bashed in.

Red spray paint or something on that order had been used to write a warning across the hood.

Death is coming.

Her heart started to pound.

Todd pulled her behind the nearest parked vehicle. "Stay down and make the call."

Her hand shook as she dragged her cell from her bag. Her fingers turned to ice as she stabbed the necessary digits and put through the call. She watched Todd move around the parking garage as she answered the dispatcher's questions. He carried a gun now. She hadn't even realized he was armed. She provided her location and explained the situation. No, as far as she could see the perpetrators were no longer on the scene. Yes, the police needed to come. No, there was no need for an ambulance. The dispatcher assured her the police were en route. Eva ended the call and absently shoved the phone back into her bag. She stretched her neck in an effort to get a look around.

There was no one else in the garage except the two of them. At least if there was, he or they were hiding. She doubted the bastards would hide. They liked to show off…to inspire fear. Scumbags.

Todd returned to her car. This time he looked inside, though he made no move to open the doors. Preserving the scene, she realized. If he touched any part of the car, he might disturb fingerprints left behind by the bad guys. Even as she considered his reasoning, he walked to the rear of her vehicle. He leaned down to inspect something in the area of the trunk and the lid suddenly sprang open. Todd disappeared behind it.

Eva's tension moved to a new level, sending her heart into her throat. She looked around. Still didn't see anyone. Before she could talk herself out of the move, she stood and started walking toward her car. She opened her mouth to call his name but her voice deserted her.

No shots rang out. No sound of scuffling or fighting. Yet, she instinctively understood that something was very, very wrong.

As she reached the hood, Todd stepped from behind the open trunk lid. "Let's go back inside until the police get here."

He was moving toward her as the words penetrated the uncertainty that had paralyzed her ability to reason. When his hand landed on her arm, she trembled. Why was he trying to urge her back inside now? Why was the trunk still open?

Sirens blared in the distance. The police

were almost here. They should stay put. Explain what happened.

"Eva," he said, his voice frighteningly soft, "I want to take you back inside."

She stared up at him. The blue eyes she knew as well as she knew her own showed no emotion...no indication of what the trouble was. And then she understood. He was hiding something terrible from her.

Her throat went as dry as bone. "What's in the trunk?"

Two police cruisers barreled into the parking garage and skidded to a stop.

Todd gripped her elbow and urged her in the direction of the nearest cruiser "I'll explain everything in a minute. Let's just make sure you stay safe until—"

Eva broke free of his grip and ran to her car. Her heart thudded so hard in her chest she couldn't catch a breath.

"Eva, wait!"

She'd spoken to Lena yesterday. She was safe in DC. Eva rounded the back of the vehicle. Fear constricted her chest. She stared into the open trunk. At first what she saw didn't register. Pink dress...ghostly pale legs. Plastic that looked shrink-wrapped around the pasty skin of the woman's face. Gray hair. White cheeks...purple lips encircled a mouth that was open wide as if gasping for air. Dull, unseeing eyes.

Mrs. Cackowski.

Chapter Five

Chicago Police Department, 10:30 a.m.

Lorena Cackowski's daughter had been notified of her mother's death. She was on her way to Chicago from New York now. The preliminary conclusion from the medical examiner was asphyxiation. The murder weapon appeared to be the plastic. Manner of death: homicide.

Todd paced the corridor outside the interview room. The two detectives had insisted on interviewing Eva and him separately. He hadn't been happy about the idea, but she had assured him that she was okay with it so he'd backed off.

How the hell could Robles order the murder of a helpless, elderly woman like that?

Sick bastards.

The way Eva had trembled, the tears pouring down her cheeks, had torn him apart. He would make Robles pay for hurting her. As much as the desire to go after that revenge burned inside him, his top priority had to be keeping Eva safe.

The door opened and Detective Marsh stepped into the corridor. "Almost done." He shook his head. "This thing is getting damned hairy."

"Who's the new guy?" Todd gestured to the interview room the man had exited. Marsh was the one to take Todd's statement but another detective had shown up for Eva's official interview. "He wasn't your partner the last time we had the pleasure of your company."

Marsh hitched his head toward the closed door. "Carter is from Gang Intelligence. He's been working this one behind the scenes since the war on Friday night. Until this morning he was more focused on what happened before Diego and his friends hit the ER. Everything's changed now."

Murder had a way of changing things for sure.

"This murder will draw a lot of press to the department," Marsh confessed.

Todd nodded. "Have the evidence techs found anything in the vic's apartment that ties Robles's people to what happened?"

For whatever reason, the usual gang markings hadn't been left behind in the vic's apartment or on Eva's car. It was possible that Robles considered this personal rather than gang business. Either way, he was behind the threats and now at least one murder related to Eva.

"Not yet," Marsh said with a weary sigh. "These guys might be thugs but the ones in charge aren't stupid. They know how to cover their tracks. Even if we're lucky enough to have witnesses we know for a fact were right there watching, they rarely talk. Too afraid, and who can blame them?"

Todd understood that the I-didn't-see-anything mentality in situations like this happened all too often. Fear was the primary motive. "I spoke with my boss. We're taking Ms. Bowman to a safe house. You have a problem with that?"

Marsh shrugged. "I think Carter is making that offer as we speak. Yours, ours, wherever she is protected works for me."

Todd was glad to hear it. "We prefer our own place. No offense."

Marsh held up his hands. "None taken. Just keep us advised."

"Will do." Todd intended to leave that part in Victoria's more-than-capable hands.

She had her own high-level sources inside Chicago PD. Todd had no reason to doubt Marsh's integrity or Carter's, for that matter. Still, he wasn't willing to take the risk that there could be a leak. Frankly, CPD had its share of problems, and he didn't intend for Eva to become a casualty of the department's recent highly publicized internal issues.

The interview room door opened once more and Eva walked out, followed by Sergeant Carter. The senior detective thrust his hand toward Todd. "We appreciate your cooperation, Christian. We'll have other questions, I'm certain. So keep us apprised of your location."

Evidently Eva had already told him the Colby Agency planned to take her to a private safe house. "You got it, Sergeant."

Eva only glanced at Todd as he spoke. Her eyes were red from crying. She kept her slender arms tight around herself. The mere idea that her life was in jeopardy was a painful reminder of just how fleeting life could be. He reached for her, placed his hand at the small of her back, hoping to convey reassurance as he guided her out of this place. The sooner they were as far as possible from the streets Robles influenced, the happier he would be.

When they had reached the lobby, he waylaid her at the main exit door and leaned in close. "Ian Michaels is picking us up. He'll drop us at the safe house. A new car will be waiting for us there. I guarantee Robles won't find us where we're going. You will be safe there."

She nodded.

Outside, Michaels waited at the curb in front of the main entrance. He glanced in the rearview mirror as they settled in the back seat.

Todd made the introductions.

"I'm aware this is a terrifying situation," Michaels said to Eva with another quick glance in the rearview mirror as he eased out onto the street, "but, rest assured, we will take care of the situation."

"Thank you."

Todd resisted the urge to scoot across the seat and put his arm around her. He was fairly confident she wouldn't appreciate the gesture however well he meant it. It would be in his best interest to stay out of her personal space for now. Keeping a couple of feet between them would be the smartest thing to do. His instincts went a little haywire when they were too close for too long.

He'd thought of her often over the years. Never expected to see her again. Even after he moved back to the Windy City, he hadn't worried. Chicago was a big place. No reason they should run into each other and be forced to deal with the lingering awkwardness. Not that he hadn't looked her up. He had. He'd checked up on her from time to time over the years before he returned to Chicago. He'd felt immensely proud when she graduated nursing school. Mostly he'd watched for an engagement announcement. Not that Eva was big on social media, but her sister, Lena, was. He'd admired the birthday pics Lena had posted each year since the last time Todd had seen Eva. He closely scrutinized the occasional vacation shot or night out on the town he ferreted out on social media. He'd scoured each one looking for the man who had taken his place.

That feeling—dread—he always experienced when he thought of her with someone else filled his chest now. *Idiot.* He'd left her because he couldn't handle where he felt the relationship was headed, and yet, he still couldn't bear the idea of her with anyone else.

He was worse than an idiot. He was a jerk.

Finding Michaels watching him in the rearview mirror warned his brooding hadn't escaped the older man's scrutiny. Ian Michaels had been with Victoria at the Colby Agency since she and her first husband started the agency. A former US Marshal, Michaels was particularly good at reading people. Todd figured the man likely already had a firm handle on how he was feeling right now.

Great.

Nothing like the world knowing how badly you'd screwed up whether it was yesterday or ten years ago.

He glanced at Eva and immediately turned his attention back to the street. He'd been a selfish bastard and he'd walked away from the only woman who had ever made him want more than right now.

Nothing he could do about the past. But he could make sure her future was free of thugs like Robles.

Bastard.

"Brace yourselves," Michaels announced. "We have a tail to lose."

THE CAR ROCKETED forward and fear trapped deep in Eva's chest.

Todd's hand was suddenly against her back, ushering her down onto the seat. He used his own body like a shield, hovering over her as the car swung from lane to lane. When he pressed more firmly against her, she started to demand what the hell he was doing, but the sound of glass shattering and metal popping silenced her.

"Hang on!"

The driver shouted the words and then slammed on the brakes. The car slid sideways. For an instant Todd's body crushed against hers, every rigid muscle cradling her. Eva's stomach lurched as much from his nearness as from the wild ride. Before she could catch her breath, the car was rocketing forward once more.

Another of those crazy sliding turns was followed by a roar of the car's engine as they zoomed through the city streets. Eva was grateful she couldn't see. No doubt pedestrians and other vehicles were scattered all around them. One wrong move and the crash would be horrific.

A moment passed with no abrupt moves and her respiration leveled out to some degree. She realized then that her fingers were clutched in the fabric of Todd's shirt. One muscled thigh had burrowed between hers, his knee anchored to the seat, holding her firmly in place. His other knee was planted in the floorboard and his upper torso shielded hers. The scent of his strong body, clean and vaguely sweet, filled her lungs and made her dizzy.

Pull yourself together, girl.

Eva took a breath and ordered her fingers to unclench. She was still working on the move when Ian Michaels announced, "All clear."

Todd's face turned down toward hers, making her breath catch all over again. "You okay?"

She nodded. Her fingers finally relaxed their death grip. Todd helped her upright once more and she struggled to right her clothes and her hair. She forced herself to breathe slowly and deeply until her heart stopped racing. She kept her gaze on the street. The rear windshield was shattered but, thankfully, remained in place.

Eva closed her eyes and told herself over and over that everything would be okay. Forty-five minutes later she still wasn't completely convinced as Mr. Michaels took an exit from I-94 toward Central Avenue in Highland Park. From there he drove to Egandale Road. Eva stared out the window at nothing at all until finally the car slowed and then stopped at a keypad outside an enormous gate. A high fence was almost completely camouflaged by mature trees and shrubbery. Michaels entered the code for the gate, rolling on through as it opened.

Todd glanced at her and smiled. "Don't worry. I've been here a couple of times before. It's not as uninviting as it looks from here. The security wall only makes it look like a prison."

As they rounded a deep bend in the long drive, Eva spotted the house. It sat in the middle of thick woods.

"Beyond all those trees," Todd said as if he'd read her mind, "is Lake Michigan. The property includes a helipad as well as a boat dock. There are plenty of ways to escape trouble if the need arises. But it would prove extremely difficult for trouble to get into the compound. The walls around the property are lined with cameras. Anyone gets close, we'll know it. A state-of-the-art security system keeps the home secure. Robles's men won't be able to get to you here."

The car came to a stop in front of an enormous house that looked more like a castle than a home. Eva stared at the stone façade that might have looked cold if not for the lush border of flowering plants, climbing vines and shrubs. "Oh my God."

Michaels looked over the seat. "Call if you need anything else."

"Will do," Todd responded as he climbed out. He was around the vehicle and opening her door before she had the presence of mind to grab her bag and prepare to exit the car.

Ian Michaels drove away in the car with its broken glass and bullet holes. Eva turned to the massive house, clinging to her leather bag as if it was the only thing left grounding her. At the moment she was pretty sure it was. This insane situation had taken her from her home, had kept her from work, and cost her neighbor her life. On cue, her head started to spin.

Todd's steady hand was suddenly at her back, ushering her up the stone steps. "All the windows are bulletproof," he explained. "A voice command can close the steel shutters over them." At the door, he placed his hand against a large pad. As soon as the system had identified him, the locks on the door released. He opened the door and waited for her to enter ahead of him.

Inside, the home was large but warmly decorated. The layout appeared user-friendly. The floors were a smooth, rich wood that flowed forward in a welcoming path. The walls were coated in an inviting beige bordered by gorgeous ornate trim drenched in a gloss white.

"There's a six-car garage with a nice selection of vehicles, all well equipped for speed and safety if we need to take a drive. Whenever the house is not in use, the agency in-vestigators take turns, on a rotating basis, spending weekends here for the sole purpose of driving the vehicles. I was here two week-ends ago. The solitude is incredibly relaxing."

As imposing as everything about the house was, there was no denying its infinite beauty. Someone had gone to a great deal of trouble to create a luxurious getaway. "Has anyone ever lived here?"

Todd shook his head. "Victoria had it built to replace the agency's former safe house."

Eva took her gaze from the stunning view out the towering windows. "Former safe house?"

"She and her first husband built a lake house shortly after starting the Colby Agency," Todd explained, "but their seven-year-old son was abducted from there, so Victoria couldn't bring herself to live in that house again."

Eva's hand went to her throat. "How awful. Did they find him?"

Todd shook his head. "No. Twenty years later, he found her. Her first husband had died years before. But Jim, the son, found his way home. He and his family live in the old lake house now. And Victoria and Lucas, her second husband, live in a gated community near there."

Eva was glad the story had a happy ending. It was too bad that Victoria's first husband hadn't lived to see his son return.

"The kitchen is stocked with anything you could want." He turned to Eva. "If you'd like to eat."

"I'm not really hungry." How could she eat? Poor Mrs. Cackowski was dead. She squeezed her eyes shut. Murdered. It didn't seem real...except she knew it was.

"Understandable," he said, drawing her attention back to him. He gestured to the staircase that wound around the far wall and up to the second floor. "Your room is the second on the left. Anything you might need during your stay has been provided."

Eva nodded. She needed some time to gather her composure. "I think I'll lie down for a while."

"I'll be close if you need me."

She nodded before moving to the stairs.

"Eva."

She turned back to him.

"I wish there was something I could say to make this crappy day better. You're hurting, I know. Feeling guilty. Blaming yourself for Mrs. Cackowski's death. But this isn't your fault. You just happened to be in the wrong place at the wrong time and got caught up in a gang war. But this will all get better. I promise."

Eva wanted to cry but she felt all cried out. She nodded and trudged up the stairs.

How would she ever face her neighbor's daughter? What words could she say to explain that the woman's death was her fault? No matter what Todd said, it was true. If Eva hadn't moved in across the hall from the sweet lady…if she hadn't killed a gang leader's brother…

Tears burning down her cheeks, she opened the second door on the left and walked into the room. The sheer size of the space distracted her for a moment, but it was another of those towering windows that drew her across the lush carpeting to the other side of the room. The view over the courtyard made her smile even as more of those tears spilled from her eyes. A pool with a gorgeous waterfall surrounded by lush shrubs and flowers. Rock paths bordered by dense greenery circled and cut across the rear property, creating a maze. If she were on vacation, this would be the perfect place to get lost.

But she wasn't on vacation. She was hiding from a murderer. Her bodyguard was a few steps away. If only Mrs. Cackowski had had a bodyguard.

Eva scrubbed the tears from her cheeks and turned her back to the window. She walked to the first of two doors. She couldn't think about that awful truth anymore. She had to be strong. Had to do whatever necessary to make this right.

So she focused on the mundane. Her room for the next few days had a generous walk-in closet. Several outfits—jeans, sweaters, slacks, blouses with matching shoes—had been hung at eye level. An ottoman sat in the center of the room. On top were a couple of nightshirts and a selection of lacy panties and bras.

Eva shook her head as she touched the tags on the items. She would have been certain they'd raided her closet if not for the product tags. The agency had gone to the trouble to purchase a mini wardrobe just like one she would have bought for herself based on what she had in her own closet. Why hadn't they just grabbed some of her stuff?

Didn't matter.

The next door led to a bathroom that would wow the most discriminating of tastes. From the hairbrush to the beauty products, she could be in her own bathroom except her entire space would fit into the tub of this one. This was very nice of Victoria. She hoped the arrangement wasn't costing Dr. Pierce a fortune.

Eva stared at her reflection. An elegant hiding place. And that was what she was doing. Hiding.

Unless the police caught Miguel Robles—and they hadn't been able to do so in more than a dozen years—or Robles killed her as he intended, this would never be over. More people could be hurt or murdered...like her sister.

How could she possibly hide like this?

She couldn't.

She owed it to Mrs. Cackowski and to herself to make sure Miguel Robles paid for his crimes. He shouldn't be allowed to get away with murdering a helpless elderly woman or anyone else. Since the police hadn't been able to get him, maybe she could. After all, she had the right kind of bait.

She was the woman who'd killed his little brother.

Miguel Robles wanted to kill her, too.

Sticking to her routine, staying out there where Robles could find her was the only way to lure him. The realization settled onto her like a massive stone crushing her chest.

It was true. All this time the police had been unable to find enough evidence against him, but she could draw him out, make him careless—because he wanted so badly to avenge his brother.

All she had to do was convince her bodyguard to go along with her plan.

Eva trembled at the thought of Todd. That part might prove the most difficult. She had noticed the look of guilt in his eyes more than once. He felt bad for having left her all those years ago. She'd gotten that message loud and clear. If he was looking to make up and to be friends, he could forget it. She could never be friends with him.

She couldn't trust herself.

Better to stay at odds with someone so dangerous to her sanity.

A pang of hunger vied for her attention. She should eat and figure out how to convince Todd that her plan was the right one. It was the least she could do for her sweet neighbor. Dr. Pierce had ordered her not to come to work today. That was okay. The truth was she needed to pull herself back together before she dared set foot out of this safe zone.

Not to mention she had her work cut out for her right here. As much as she would love to pretend she could do what needed to be done on her own, she was smarter than that. She needed Todd's full cooperation.

She smoothed a hand over her clothes, tugged the loosening clip from her hair and finger combed it. Steadying herself, she took a big breath and exited the luxurious bedroom. Downstairs she wandered from room to room until she found Todd. To her surprise, he was scooping vanilla ice cream into a bowl.

"I seem to recall you were a chocolate man." She moved to the massive island in the center of the room and propped herself there.

"Don't worry." He licked the scoop and set it aside. "That's coming." He reached for a jar and spooned chocolate onto the mound of creamy vanilla ice cream. "Join me."

"I think I'll see what else is available."

He moaned, drawing her attention to his lips as he withdrew the chocolate-smeared spoon from his mouth. "You should rethink that strategy. The latest philosophy on the art of eating is that having dessert first is better."

"Maybe for a guy who's solid muscle." She opened the glass door of the double fridge. "Not for a girl who has to watch every ounce of fat she eats settle on her hips and thighs."

The salad fixings in the crisper drawer would work. She gathered the bag of greens, a basket of tomatoes and the vinaigrette dressing. She pushed the door closed with her hip.

"I don't see anything wrong with your hips or your thighs."

Eva looked from him to her lower anatomy. "I've come to appreciate how scrubs can cover a multitude of sins."

"Somehow I doubt there are any sins to hide." He shoveled another spoonful of chocolate-covered ice cream into his mouth. Chocolate dripped down his chin.

Looking away, she plopped her load on the counter and searched for a plate. As hard as she tried to focus on preparing her salad and ignoring him, her gaze kept shifting over to see if he'd swiped that chocolate from his chin.

Finally, when she couldn't take it any longer, she grabbed a napkin and walked over to him, then held it out. "You have chocolate… on your chin."

Rather than take the napkin he grabbed her hand—the one clasping the napkin—and swiped at his chin. The stubble there tickled her fingers and made her breath hitch.

"Did I get it?"

She drew her hand from the clutch of his long fingers. "Yes."

Leaving the napkin on the counter in front of him, she walked back to her salad.

"I'm telling you—" she glanced back at him as he spoke "—I don't see anything that's not exactly right with those hips."

She flashed a fake smile. "Thanks."

Determined to pretend his words, his voice—his mere presence—were not turning her inside out, she placed the grape tomatoes atop the bed of Italian mixed greens and then added the dressing. As she twisted the top back on the bottle, she realized she needed something crunchy. Crackers, croutons. Something.

A bag of croutons landed on the counter next to her plate. Todd grinned. "You always liked some crunch with your salads."

"Thanks." Evidently they both remembered plenty about each other. But there was one thing she could not afford to forget. Todd Christian had stolen her heart and then he'd left it shattered on the doorstep when he walked away.

She had every confidence she could trust him completely with her life…but he could not be trusted in any capacity with her heart.

Chapter Six

Eva pushed to her limit. The grinding *whir* of the treadmill was the only sound in the room. She'd explored the entire house and decided a walk outside would do her good. Except Todd had insisted on accompanying her if she was setting one foot outside the house.

She'd wanted to shake him and inform him that her goal was to get as far away from him as possible. But that attitude wouldn't be conducive to cooperation.

A quick call to her friend Kim Levy had confirmed that they were shorthanded in the ER. Eva would use that as her first negotiating tactic. She doubted that particular tactic would carry much weight with her bodyguard, but it was a starting place. Then she had gone online and done extensive research on the True Disciples. She raised the incline on the treadmill and forced her exhausted body to comply. This well-equipped exercise room wasn't the only amenity in the Colby safe house. There was an office with three computers and the fastest internet access speed she had ever encountered, making her search all the easier.

She had discovered that Miguel Robles had been arrested no less than a dozen times but not once had the police been able to make it stick. He and his followers were thought to be involved in drug trafficking and gun smuggling across the northern border. Numerous murders were attributed to their ranks. Occasionally one or more of the followers would end up with a rap they couldn't escape. In each instance the gang member accepted his fate and never said a word. Deal after deal had been offered to lure in the "big fish" and not one of Robles's followers had accepted.

The elder Robles was more than the average thug. He was smart and he surrounded himself with above-average intelligence when it came to the highest level within or affiliated with his organization. Everyone from his CPA and his personal physician to the lawyers who represented him were from the city's most esteemed ranks. Just went to show what even an intelligent person with reasonable ethical standards would do for money.

Bottom line, she needed a better-than-average plan. An ordinary person like her couldn't hope to win a battle against Miguel Robles unless she had something extraordinary to offer.

Like the woman responsible for the death of his only brother.

She slowed the track speed and lowered the incline. Five miles was plenty to clock, particularly since she hadn't managed even a mile since last Friday. A few more minutes at a comfortable walk and her respiration was back to normal and she was ready to hit Stop. Eva grabbed her hand towel, patted her damp face and neck and headed for a shower. Maybe she would find an opening at dinner to discuss her concerns regarding her responsibilities at work. Other than her sister, her career was all she had. Though Dr. Pierce was onboard with her current dilemma, she doubted he would feel that way a month from now. He certainly wouldn't want to bankroll her situation forever.

Dragging out the inevitable wasn't going to alleviate this situation.

In the hall, she ran headlong into her bodyguard. She stumbled back in surprise, her fatigued muscles instantly reacting to the hard contours of his. "Sorry." She cleared her throat to buy time to steady herself. "I was lost in thought."

A bone-melting smile stretched across his lips. "Looks like you showed that treadmill who's boss."

"Ha, ha." She dabbed at her forehead.

His gaze slid down her body, lingering on her legs before returning to her face. The fitted running leggings were a little too well fitted, but there hadn't been anything else suitable for her workout in the provided wardrobe. The tank wasn't much better. Far tinier and tighter than she felt comfortable wearing with him around. The running shoes were high-end, and her size, and inordinately comfortable. As long as she was stuck here with him, she intended to spend as much time in the gym as possible. Alone, preferably.

Yet, deep down she understood that all the workouts in the world would not stop *this* inevitability either if she remained holed up with him for too long.

If she was lucky she would be able to talk him into going along with her plan sooner rather than later.

"Dinner's ready."

"You made dinner?" She didn't know why

she was surprised. He made dinner for her often…before. She'd assumed that was only because he had his own apartment and she lived in the dorm. Preparing dinner at home for a date was certainly cheaper than taking her to a restaurant. All that aside, he'd been a decent cook.

"Don't get excited," he warned. "It's only spaghetti."

"As long as there's a salad I'll be in heaven." At home and at work she popped more spaghetti dinners in the microwave than she would want to admit. It was the one sure-fire frozen entrée she could count on.

"Take your shower. I'll put together a salad and some garlic bread and track down a bottle of wine."

He flashed another of those charming smiles and goose bumps spread over her skin. She nodded and hurried to the stairs, putting distance between them as quickly as she could without breaking into a run. After finding Mrs. Cackowski murdered, the wine sounded like the best part of dinner. She could definitely use a glass to help her relax. But she had no desire to make herself even more vulnerable to Todd—especially *alone* with him.

Between the hard run and the luxuriously

long shower, she felt immensely better. It never ceased to amaze her how much working out helped adjust her outlook. Hopefully, that good, confident outlook would help with what she had to do next.

Todd was heaping sauce onto a bed of noodles on a plate when she walked into the kitchen. He glanced up. "Have a seat. I'll serve."

A memory flashed through her mind, making her step falter. The image of her naked on his dining table, warm spaghetti sauce slipping down her skin, over her breasts… followed by his tongue lapping up the spicy sauce. He'd come to the living room to drag her to the kitchen to eat. She'd been waiting for him—naked and ready for more than just dinner. Together they'd removed his clothes on the way back into the kitchen. They'd had sex and eaten and had sex again…and snacked off each other's skin. He'd poured wine into her belly button and lapped it up, including the streams that slid well below her belly button.

Eva blinked away the memory and pressed onward to the table. This was not *that* table. This was not *that* house. Here and now was not who they *once* were.

He placed the loaded plate in front of her,

then reached the wine bottle toward her glass and started to pour. "Say when."

She snapped out of her haze and held up a hand. "That's more than enough."

When he'd moved away, she reached for the fork and the small salad bowl he'd left by her plate. She picked at the one thing on the menu that didn't remind her of sex with Todd.

"Do you remember that time—"

"I don't know." Her gaze snapped to his.

He laughed as he filled his wine glass. "I haven't told you which time I meant."

She poked a forkful of greens into her mouth.

"We stood in line at that Italian restaurant in the pouring rain." He laughed. "It had just opened and everyone said it was the best in the country."

A laugh bubbled into her throat before she could stop it. She swallowed to prevent choking, then washed it down with a long gulp of wine. "I remember. I told you if it wasn't the best *bigoli* pasta I'd ever eaten I was going to make you regret that forty-five-minute, soaked-to-the-bone wait."

They both laughed for a minute but when their gazes locked, the laughter died. Their clothes had dripped onto the wood floor of the restaurant as they'd eaten. They'd laughed and stared directly into each other's eyes through the entire meal and then they'd hurried home to make love. Eva exiled the memories and reached for her glass again. A long gulp of wine later, she told herself to slow down. She picked at her salad a little longer before moving on to the spaghetti. It certainly did not help that images from their previous spaghetti-eating escapes kept flashing in her head.

"Did you discover anything interesting about Miguel Robles?"

Her head came up at his question. How did he know? "You monitored my online activities?"

He ducked his head. "It's my job. What kind of bodyguard would I be if I didn't pay attention to what you're doing?"

She wanted to be angry but couldn't muster up the wherewithal. "I learned more than I wanted to know," she confessed. She might as well say what was on her mind. "The police haven't been able to stop him or even come close to trapping him. Whenever they close in on some charge, someone else always takes the fall—if there's even a fall involved."

"Robles is no fool." Todd picked up his glass of water and downed a swallow.

Eva hadn't noticed until then that he had

scarcely touched his wine, reaching for the water goblet more often than not. She felt a little woozy. Clearly that was what she should have done. She'd intended to keep a clear head...but those damned memories had taken her by surprise and dragged her down a too-familiar path.

"So," she set her fork aside, "what's the plan from here? If the police don't get him, and they haven't shown any sign of success so far, what do we do?"

"We've got people working on finding a weak link."

Eva wanted to believe that was good news but honestly she didn't see how. "I'm think-ing he's the kind of man who either wins or he dies. No in between."

TODD STARED AT her and this time he reached for his wine. He knew better than to have even one glass when he was on duty, but he hadn't been able to help himself. She'd wanted some distance—that part had been clear. So he'd left her alone and watched over her shoulder via the sophisticated camera system in the house. He'd watched her search the web for information about Robles. He'd watched the worry on her face, the way she gnawed on her bottom lip as she read the stories that all—every damned one—ended badly.

Then she'd decided on a workout. He'd almost lost his mind watching her supple body move in that formfitting outfit. Finding something to occupy his mind and his hands had been necessary. Somewhere in the back of his brain some neuron misfire had sent him down memory lane with an Italian menu. It wasn't until she walked into the kitchen that he'd remembered dripping that sauce on her bare skin and licking it off. Sitting at this table for the past half hour and remembering what they had done on his table had driven him out of his mind. He was so damned hard that at the moment he might not be able to stand without embarrassing himself.

He shrugged in response to her statement. "He's smart."

"We've established that he's smart," she sniped. "The question is, what are we going to do about it?" She finished off her wine. "I can't live like this forever. I have a career. I'm needed at the ER. They're shorthanded today because I'm not there. And what about Lena? She'll be coming home in a few days. How do we protect her from this insane man?"

"I see where you're going with this." He

stood and grabbed his plate. He'd lost his appetite as well as his raging erection.

By the time he reached the sink she was right behind him with her own plate in hand. "Then you know there's no other option. The police won't be able to stop him. You can't take down a bad guy without evidence. Their hands are tied. He'll just allow some low man in the gang hierarchy to take the fall for Mrs. Cackowski's murder—assuming his people can be tied to the scene. My sister, my friends—no one around me—will be safe until *he* is stopped. Mrs. Cackowski deserves justice."

He took her plate from her hand and put it in the sink with his own, then strode back to the table. His frustration level was way out of control. "What makes you think the Colby Agency can do anything—besides provide protection—more than the police are already doing? More important, what is it you believe you can do?"

"That's easy. The police want to charge him with one or more of his crimes. They want to prosecute him and see that he goes away for the rest of his life. We can help make that happen."

Todd's hands stilled on the bowl of sauce and the platter of pasta he'd intended to put away. His eyes fixed on hers. "You want to put yourself at risk."

She nodded, the move stilted. "Whatever it takes."

"Christ, Eva. You know we can't do that." He plopped the food back onto the table and set his hands on his hips. She was talking about sacrificing herself—sending a sheep to slaughter. "I don't ever want to hear you talk that way again."

"This is a war," she reasoned. "In wartime a soldier does whatever necessary to stop the enemy, right? This is the same thing. We have to draw him out or he'll just lay low and keep getting away with all manner of heinous crimes."

He shook his head. "Even in wartime there are rules of engagement, and protecting every single soldier in the field is priority one."

"If he isn't stopped, he'll just keep killing people. He won't stop until someone kills him. Since we can't exactly do that, we can at least help take him down." He opened his mouth to argue and she held up a hand. "I will not sit back and risk my sister's life or those of my friends. If that's what you expect—for me to do nothing and wait—then you can just take me home right now."

Rather than argue with her, he picked up

the food again and headed for the counter. Maybe the wine had gone to her head. She damned sure hadn't eaten much today. He busied himself with putting the leftovers away and loading the dishwasher.

The problem was she was right. Miguel Robles would not stop until he'd accomplished his goal. That was his MO. He wasn't the sort of man to walk away. Too much was riding on his ability to maintain a show of strength and power. The first sniff of weakness and his loyal disciples would eat him alive.

Eva watched him, her arms crossed over her chest, anger sparking in those green eyes of hers. "You know I'm right. All the police need is a decent opportunity to get to him. I can help make that happen. For Mrs. Cackowski." Tears glistened in her eyes.

"Let me think about it." The delay tactic likely wouldn't buy him much time, but it was the best he could do at the moment. He hadn't expected her to come out of the corner she found herself in wanting to dive into battle—at least not this early in the war.

Maybe she'd been right when she told him she wasn't the same naive girl she'd been ten years ago. He sighed. Which only made him want her more.

Idiot.

"You have until morning," she warned as she backed away from him. "FYI—tomorrow I'm going back to work. Hiding isn't the answer."

Chapter Seven

"Heart rate is 119. Respiration 39. BP is 90 over 60," Eva reported, her voice carrying above the sound of the gurney's wheels rolling as the EMT and paramedic pushed the patient through the emergency entry doors.

Dr. Arnold Reagan met them just inside. "Trauma room one," he ordered.

Another nurse, Kim Levy, as well as a respiratory tech joined Eva in trauma room one, taking over the patient from the two paramedics who'd delivered the young girl via ambulance. Kim checked the patient's airway and began the insertion of a trach tube.

"She's nineteen," the paramedic said as he backed toward the door. "She was walking to class. Witnesses said the vehicle carrying the shooter never slowed down."

"Alyssa Chavez," his partner added before they left to take another call.

Eva exchanged a look with Kim a split second before Reagan parted the already-torn blouse and had a look at the patient's chest. The bullet had entered center chest. Reagan swore. Their patient was in serious respiratory distress and profound hemorrhagic shock. If the internal bleeding wasn't stopped quickly, she would exsanguinate.

In the next two minutes the patient was readied and rushed to the OR. A surgeon was already standing by. Every second counted. Her life was literally slipping away in a far too rapid stream.

Eva stripped off her gloves, her adrenaline receding swiftly, leaving her weak.

The cell phone strapped to her ankle vibrated. She started to ignore it but decided it might be her sister. At this point she didn't dare ignore a call from anyone she cared about. Why hadn't she checked on her neighbor when she first noticed something was off? Maybe if she'd… *Stop, Eva.* It was too late for what-ifs. Finding justice for Mrs. Cackowski and all the others that bastard Robles had hurt was the one thing Eva could do.

A frown furrowed across her brow at the

number on the caller ID. Not one she recognized. She answered with a tentative, "Hello."

"Alyssa Chavez is on you, Ms. Bowman. How many more do you want to die for you?"

The call ended.

Eva stared at the phone, her heart pounding harder and harder against her sternum. The caller had been male with a slight Hispanic accent. She stared at the blood-stained instruments on the tray…the pile of bloody gloves and sheets on the floor…the disarray in the trauma room that told the story of desperation.

A young woman was fighting for her life and that was her fault.

Eva wheeled and stormed out of the trauma room. This was enough. If that woman died…

"Eva."

She stalled and turned to the man who had spoken. *Dr. Pierce*. Her chest had grown so tight she could hardly catch a breath. "Sir?"

"When you've finished here, I'd like to see you in my office."

For a moment she wasn't sure how to respond. Flashbacks from those moments under his desk staring at the sleek leather shoes and the creased trousers joined the images of the man she had killed, her dead neighbor stuffed into her trunk and a beautiful young woman bleeding out on a gurney in front of her.

Please, God, don't let her die.

"Of course. Give me five minutes."

Dr. Pierce nodded and walked away. Eva stared after him, her head still spinning. When she'd managed to slow her thrashing heart, she washed up and headed to the station.

"You okay?" Kim glanced at her from the computer monitor she was bent over. "She might make it, you know."

Eva managed a stilted nod. "Hope so. Okay isn't something I'll be anytime soon." She heaved a big breath. "Dr. Pierce wants to see me in his office."

Kim considered her for several seconds. When Eva offered no further explanation, her friend and colleague said, "We're okay for now. See what Pierce wants and then take a break." She jerked her head toward the department exit. "Go."

"I'll be back in five."

She should let Todd know about the call. He would need to inform the detectives on the case. Eva wasn't sure exactly where he was. He'd said he would be close, watching. There hadn't been time for her to wonder where or how he'd intended to do so. She hurried toward the corridor that led to the administrator's office. Her thoughts were rushing about in her head, a mishmash of worry and fear and desperation. The words the caller had said to her kept ringing in her ears. What she'd said to Todd last night had been right. Robles wouldn't stop unless he was behind bars—and maybe not even then.

How could she go on with her life and pretend Robles wasn't watching and waiting for the opportunity to snatch her or someone close to her off the street? If she persisted in her efforts to hide from him or to keep a stumbling block, i.e. her bodyguard, in Robles's path, he would only continue hurting innocent people like poor Mrs. Cackowski and Alyssa Chavez. Tears crowded into her throat.

Pull it together, Eva. She couldn't do what needed to be done if she fell apart.

Eva reached the lobby outside Pierce's office but his secretary was not at her desk. His door stood open so Eva walked to the opening and knocked once on the doorframe. Pierce looked up and motioned for her to come inside.

"Close the door."

Her hands shaking now despite every effort she attempted to keep them steady, she closed the door and crossed to his desk, then she waited for further instructions.

He glanced up, gestured to the chair in front of his desk. "Have a seat."

Had Pierce changed his mind about having her back at work? Had he already heard about the phone call? Impossible. She hadn't told anyone...but maybe the man who'd called her—presumably Robles—had called the administrator as well.

"Dr. Pierce, if you've changed your mind about my being here, I completely understand. Especially after what just happened." Eva squeezed her eyes shut a moment. "I am so sorry for what I've caused." More of that humiliating emotion gathered in her eyes. Where was her professional decorum?

He studied her for a moment, confusion lining his brow. "I'm not sure what you're talking about, Eva."

She met his questioning gaze. "A man called me right before you asked me to your office. He said..." She moistened her lips and wished she could swallow the lump of agony lodged in her throat. "He said Alyssa Chavez was on me." Deep breath. "It's my fault she was shot."

The tears burst onto her lashes and streamed down her cheeks before she could stop them.

And she'd thought she was strong. Pierce grabbed a box of tissue and came around to sit beside her. He offered the box to her. "Have you notified Detective Marsh or spoken with Mr. Christian?"

Feeling more foolish than she had in years, she shook her head. "It just happened. I was going to after our meeting. I understand if you'd rather I didn't come back to work until this is...over."

Over? Would it ever be over as long as she was breathing?

"We need you here," he said, his voice un-characteristically gentle.

Eva dabbed at her eyes. "My being here puts everyone in danger." She should have thought of that—she should also have re-alized that she was operating on emotion. Never a good thing.

"Your work here is what ultimately put you in this position, Eva. As a member of my staff I have an obligation to you. We've beefed up security. I can assure you that none of those thugs are getting in again. I'm fairly confi-dent this Miguel Robles will keep hurting people in an attempt to get to you no matter where you are. If you'd been at home today that poor young woman may have ended up on your doorstep."

She couldn't argue with him there. Mrs. Cackowski was proof of his conclusion. The mere thought of how she'd looked stuffed into that trunk as if she were a worthless object rather than a lovely human being made her want to break down completely.

Eva took a steadying breath and gathered her scattered composure. "I appreciate your understanding. So, why did you want to speak with me?"

"I have a question about that night." The gentle tone was gone now. He sounded more like the commanding hospital administrator she had come to know.

"What would you like to know?" Her heart started that runaway galloping again. Did he somehow know she had lied to him about being in his office that night? Damn it, why hadn't she simply told him the truth in the first place?

You weren't thinking straight, Eva.

"You're certain you didn't see anyone come into or out of my office while you were in hiding?"

Damn. There it was. To reaffirm the lie was her first instinct. She hesitated. Lying to the man who was basically the only reason she had anyone watching over her in all this was simply wrong. She owed it to him to tell the truth. For what it was worth, at any rate.

"I wasn't completely forthcoming with you that night, Dr. Pierce." She shook her head and stared at her hands. "I was so shaken by what happened, I wasn't thinking clearly."

"I need you to start at the beginning and tell me exactly what happened after you left the ladies' room."

The sternness in his tone warned that he was not happy to hear her confession. Of course he wasn't happy. She had lied to the man who had given everything to designing and creating the most cutting-edge emergency department in the country. He had chosen his staff carefully and she'd just let him down. It would be a miracle if she still had a job when this meeting was over.

"I went into your office like you told me to do, but I heard someone coming so I hid in the first available space I spotted—under your desk." She braced for spilling the rest. "I hoped it was you coming to tell me everything was okay, but it wasn't."

He waited, silent, staring at her with an intensity that sent her composure fleeing once more.

"All I saw were his shoes and his trouser legs. Based on what I heard, he at first seemed to move around your office rifling through things, then he came to your desk. He opened each drawer and then I heard him scrawl something on your desk blotter." Her mouth had gone as dry as a box of fresh cotton balls.

"Did he take anything from the drawers?"

She shook her head. "Not that I saw. He pulled each one open, rummaged through the contents and then pushed it close."

"Did it seem as though he might be photographing anything?"

Eva had to think about that one. "I don't think so. When he walked in he moved around the room without really stopping. He seemed in a hurry, maybe. At the desk... I suppose he might have photographed something during the few seconds before he started to open the drawers."

"He didn't say anything. Make a phone call?"

She shook her head again. "He just left that message."

I know what you did.

Pierce's silence added another layer of tension to the band already twisting tighter around her chest.

"Do you have any questions about that message?"

For the second time since she entered his office the urge to lie rushed to the tip of her tongue, but she resisted. "I'm certain you would tell me if there was a reason I needed to know."

"Eva." He exhaled a heavy breath. "When you create something everyone wants before anyone else can do so, you put yourself in a position to suffer extreme backlash and jealousy. Creating this unprecedented facility and launching a successful operation came at great professional and personal cost. Manufacturers of any medical product that is not used in this facility despise me. Most of the colleagues I once considered friends resent me. My efforts to do good have produced many enemies."

She'd had no idea how difficult his journey had been, though she did understand. Her sister's rising stardom as an investigative journalist had come at a high price. She'd lost lifelong friends and was as lonely as Eva. Just another confirmation that it was impossible to have it all. How sad that a man like Pierce had been forced to give up so much to create something so valuable to mankind.

"Don't waste your sympathy on me," he said, reading her face. "I executed more than my share of cutthroat maneuvers to make my success happen."

Eva felt so foolish now about the hasty decision she'd made to withhold the truth that terrifying night. "I apologize for not telling you everything. What I heard and saw didn't feel important considering the other events playing out so I dismissed the entire episode." A pretty pathetic excuse but it was the truth.

"Tell me about his shoes, Eva."

Surprised but determined to provide the best answer possible, she turned over the image in her mind. "Dark, black I think. Leather for sure. Not the off-the-shelf kind you find in a big chain department store. These were expensive shoes. The trousers, too. They were like a charcoal or dark gray color and creased as if he'd just, you know, gotten them from the cleaners."

"Tell me about his hand. You said you watched him open the drawers. Was he wearing a ring of any sort or a watch? Did you see his shirtsleeve? If so, what color shirt was he wearing? Cuff links?"

His rapid-fire questions reminded her of the interview with Detective Marsh and his partner. Had something else happened that may have been headed off if she'd told him the truth in the first place?

One more thing to feel guilty about.

Eva closed her eyes and replayed the moments in her head. Light gray shirtsleeve to go with the darker gray trousers. She told Pierce as much. "There was a watch. No ring that I saw. No cuff links."

"What did the watch look like? Gold? Silver? An expensive brand?"

"Silver. Average size. Black face, I think. I couldn't see the brand but it looked heavy, expensive."

"Thank you, Eva. If you recall anything else, please let me know." He checked his cell. "By the way, the girl—Alyssa Chavez—is holding her own in surgery. I'll assign a security detail to her room when she comes out of surgery."

Relief swam through Eva's veins. "Thank God." She stood. "I'm not scheduled for the next two days. If you change your mind about me coming in on Sunday—"

"I won't."

"Thank you, sir."

As she exited the lobby area, Eva met his secretary, Patricia Ezell. The older woman smiled as if she understood the relief no doubt painting Eva's face. Once she reached the corridor she spotted the other possibility for the secretary's smile.

Todd Christian leaned against the wall, the nondescript tan scrubs taking not one ounce of masculinity away from him. How was it possible for any man to look that good in scrubs?

As she reached him, he pushed away from the wall. "I was hoping you'd give me a tour of the cafeteria. I hear it's the best hospital food in the city."

The tension that had held her in its ruthless grip as she entered Pierce's office eased, only to be replaced by a new kind of tension.

"It's good, yes. I just have to check in with the desk and then maybe I can take a lunch break."

He walked with her toward the ER. She tuned out the subtle scent of his soap. She should not have noticed the earthy, muted smell over the more potent odors of the hospital, and yet somehow she did.

"I received an unsettling phone call after the shooting victim, Alyssa Chavez, was taken to the OR," she told him, ready to get the painful business over. For the first time she wondered how Robles had her cell number? Who was she kidding? A scumbag like that probably had all sorts of unsavory resources.

"Robles?" He glanced at her, no surprise in his eyes. "I take it she was another message."

Eva nodded. "He said she was on me and asked how many more I wanted to die for me."

He stalled then, turned to her, one hand automatically going to her arm and squeezing reassuringly. "He wants you to feel as if this is your fault, but it's not. I'll call Marsh and let him know. Would you like me to take you back to the safe house? I'm sure Pierce will understand."

"No." She squared her shoulders and gave her head a quick shake. "I'm not going to be bullied by him. I'm here. I'm staying. Maybe before I come back on Sunday this will be behind me."

Those long fingers of his tightened on her arm once more. "We'll get him."

"Hope so."

They started walking once more and he said, "You were pretty awesome when the girl came in." He glanced at her, a big, wide smile on his face. "I liked watching you work."

"I didn't see you."

"I stayed out of the way. You were focused."

As they entered the emergency department, Eva couldn't deny a sense of pride at his words. "This is a good team. I'm lucky to be a part of it."

"I'm reasonably sure they know how lucky they are to have you as well."

She doubted Alyssa Chavez was feeling lucky. That massive cloud of doom that had disappeared for a few minutes was back. "Maybe."

Kicking aside the worry, she let Kim know she was taking an early lunch break. She and Todd could call Marsh together. Eva wanted to know what progress they had made on the case. The sooner they could tie all this to Robles, the sooner this would be over.

Except she wasn't holding her breath on that last part.

Robles wanted her and she had a bad, bad feeling nothing the police could do would change his mind.

This war was intensely private.

Eva had spent four years in college learning how and the past six working hard to save lives. For the first time in her life she contemplated the concept of taking one.

Chapter Eight

Colby Safe House, 9:30 p.m.

Todd did a perimeter check and then another walk-through of the house. Though it was doubtful anyone or thing could get past the security system without him knowing about it, another look never hurt.

Mainly because he needed to distract himself.

He'd spent twelve hours today watching Eva. Every move, every word…she didn't breathe without him knowing how deep. He'd kept as much distance as he dared, which was necessary on more than one level, but he'd stayed close enough to intervene if there was trouble. Other than the Chavez woman who'd served as a message from Robles, the day had been reasonably uneventful.

But watching her, listening to her voice, catching the occasional smile, had slowly but surely escalated the tension building inside him to the point of snapping. He had vivid memories of how her skin felt beneath his touch…how it smelled, tasted…but none of those memories held a candle to the real thing. Watching her was driving him out of his mind.

He shoved the last of the dinnerware into the dishwasher. When she'd announced that she was calling it a night early he'd almost hugged her in gratitude. Another few minutes and he would have undoubtedly said or done something he would regret. His self-control had long ago reached the breaking point.

Ten years was a long time to measure every woman he met, every kiss, every touch by the one he let go. He had no one else to blame for his misery…but he just hadn't been ready for the kind of commitment she deserved.

Or maybe he had been afraid he didn't deserve her.

What had a guy like him possessed to offer such an amazing woman? His parents had abandoned him and his little brother. His mother had died from the drugs she couldn't let go of and his father from a car accident— at least that was what he'd heard. He'd grown up in foster care. The last family who'd taken him in as a rebellious teenager had been good to him. He'd treated them the way he had all the others—with total indifference. Still, they hadn't given up. If he'd learned anything from those caring folks it was that his future was his to make. They'd drilled the importance of an education and a career into his head. With their encouragement, he'd made it to college. Then he'd met Eva and fallen head over heels…but how could he trust himself to do right by her when all that he'd known growing up was instability and one letdown after the other?

No matter that those last couple of years before college he'd found a good home, he could not trust himself to do the right thing. So he'd given every part of himself to her physically but he'd kept his emotional distance. Or so he'd thought at the time.

He had spent the decade since he left Chicago proving and establishing his worth. Achieving financial security. Devoted to his country at first, then back to the city that was home. As much heartache as he'd endured growing up in the Windy City, he had every right to walk away and never look back. But the truth was, Eva was still here. Not once in all this time had he admitted that part to himself. Building the life he wanted to share with someone one day had been his ultimate goal.

The sad part was he hadn't found anyone else with whom he wanted to share that life. The past year he'd felt satisfied just sharing the city with Eva and waiting for her to marry some great guy who deserved her. Maybe then he could get on with his life.

Except she hadn't settled down with some other man.

When her file had been passed around at the agency's Monday morning briefing, Todd felt as if he'd been punched in the gut. He'd seen the news on Saturday about the incident at the Edge but her name hadn't been mentioned. As shocked as he'd been to learn she was involved and in danger, none of it had carried the impact of seeing her up close.

Yeah, he'd watched her a couple of times. Always from a safe distance. Educating himself on her life since he left her, keeping up with who she dated—none of it had adequately prepared him for standing in the same room with her. Watching her in the trauma room with that young woman who'd been shot had shifted something inside him. Her intense focus, capable hands and sincere care for the patient had made him fall for her all over again, only this time it was way beyond physical.

He now also fully understood he was in trouble.

He wanted to do far more than keep her safe. He wanted to touch her. He wanted to relearn every inch of her. He wanted to taste her...to hear her cry his name. He wanted her to belong to him.

Truly crazy, Christian.

An hour or so ago she had announced she needed a long hot bath and disappeared into her suite, and he had been trying to distract himself since. From time to time he checked the monitor. Looked without looking, so to speak. She was safe. In the bathroom there was no video, only audio. Just listening to her moans of satisfaction and the *drip, drip, drip* of the water had made him hard.

With the kitchen cleaned up, the perimeter and all egresses checked, he might as well hit the gym. Maybe he could burn off some of this excess adrenaline. Either that or he was going to explode. He hesitated at the door to her bedroom. His fingers fisted. She wouldn't want to hear about how badly he wanted her or how much he wished he could go back and have a do-over of the past.

He went into his own room—just across the hall—and peeled off his clothes. He tossed the scrubs on the bed and dug up a pair of running shorts and a tee. Once his sneakers were on, he hustled down the stairs. The best way to hammer down this kind of frustration was to run long and fast on an extreme incline setting. By the time he finished his body would be too physically spent for anything else.

He would defeat this need if it killed him.

Eva STARED AT her reflection as she set the hair dryer and brush aside. The ER had been hectic all afternoon. Nothing as serious as a gunshot but more than their fair share of automobile accidents, work-related injuries and falls. The last patient who'd come in, an elderly woman who'd broken an arm falling down the stairs in her building's stairwell, had kept Eva an hour past the end of her shift. The lady had wanted Eva at her side every step of the way until she was released. Eva wouldn't have left her for anything. She'd teared up more than once thinking about how she hadn't been there for her sweet neighbor.

Can't change that painful reality.

The best news of the day was that Alyssa Chavez was going to make it. The surgery had been a success. Her family had arrived to be with her. Between the newly increased security at the Edge and Chicago PD, no one other than staff and family were getting anywhere near her room.

Detective Marsh and his new partner from Gang Intelligence, Sergeant Carter, were less than thrilled with the news that someone— probably Miguel Robles—had contacted Eva and claimed responsibility for the shooting. She suspected their plates were already more than full. Piling on another incident, particularly a shooting, was not helpful. For Eva it confirmed her most troubling conclusion: Robles had no intention of stopping until he'd gotten his revenge.

She turned away from the mirror and the weary reflection there. She'd dried her hair and pulled on a pair of the provided PJs. These were comfortable lounge pants with a matching tank-style tee. The pale pink color was one of her favorites. She wished she had nail polish and a couple of emery boards and she'd give herself a manicure and pedicure. Not that she really needed one or even wanted one but it would buy some time. Still too early for bed. Mostly she was too keyed up to dare lie down now. Spending a couple of hours tossing and turning was her least favorite thing to do.

Maybe she should have spent a little longer on the treadmill. No matter that her arms and legs felt like limp noodles, especially after the hot bath, the tension and frustrating anticipation hung on like a bad migraine.

Surrendering, she decided to take her towel and the day's clothes to the laundry room and then she intended to find a bottle of wine. Going for something stronger wouldn't be smart. Wine would do the trick without making her potentially do something stupid—as long as she stayed in her room and clear of any possibility of running into him. Being locked away alone in a house with Todd was asking for serious trouble.

It was silent downstairs. Images played across the television screen but the sound was muted. The main hall that cut through the center of the house was cool and quiet. No sign of Todd. The kitchen proved the same. Almost there. The laundry room was deserted, too.

She sorted her laundry into the labeled hampers. A cleaning team came in each day and took care of laundry and whatever else was needed. She imagined a clearance and a thorough background search were required of the team. Just giving them access to the property meant they were above reproach. As much as she hated doing laundry, she wouldn't want to live like this. The house and property were beautiful but far too grand for her taste. She liked simple and homey.

The security part didn't actually bother her. Dr. Pierce was equally careful with his staff at the Edge. No one worked there without a flawless background. She found it near unbelievable that someone had managed to reach his office without being stopped. Then again, security had been focused on the events unfolding in the emergency department. There were cameras everywhere as well. Why hadn't the intruder been captured on camera? Maybe that was the reason for all the questions about what he had been wearing.

Eva had a feeling the man and his message were intensely personal to Dr. Pierce. Whatever it was, it went well beyond professional. Not that she was in the position to judge. Her life was wacked out on all levels. Her primary goal at this point was surviving—what she knew she had to do in order to stop Robles.

Without incident, she found the wine cellar that wasn't really a cellar but a climate-controlled room. Wherever Todd was he had so far stayed out of her path. She was grateful. There were hundreds of bottles on display in the wine room. Control pads showed the temperature and humidity level in the various glass-encased storage shelves. She moved through the rows of white and blush wines until she found something sweet and bubbly.

Back in the kitchen she prowled through the drawers until she found a new-model corkscrew that made opening a bottle of wine easy. When the cork popped free, she grabbed the bottle by the neck and a glass by the stem and headed back to the stairs. She'd made it all the way to the bottom of the staircase when she sensed his presence. A shiver rushed over her skin.

"Taking a friend to bed I see."

His voice held a teasing quality but there was something else she couldn't quite discern. She glanced over her shoulder to say good-night but the sight of him stopped her. He wore nothing but running shorts. The loose kind that rode high on his muscled thighs and low on his lean belly. The tee he'd been wearing was wadded in his hand and serving as a mop for his glistening chest.

The bottle in her hand felt suddenly too heavy. Her fingers tightened around it. She did the same with the glass. "Good night," she somehow managed.

Go. Now.

The words were her mantra as she climbed the stairs. The need to look back at him burned in her brain but she refused. He watched her until she disappeared beyond his view. She didn't have to look back to know he'd been watching her. She'd felt his gaze burning into her…smelled the devastatingly sexy scent of his clean sweat.

The instant she was in her room with the door closed, she poured a hefty serving of wine into her glass and downed it. She did the same with a second glass and had just poured a third when she heard the door across the hall slam.

She closed her eyes and sipped at the third glass. However hard she fought to banish the images, the events unfolding across the hall slowly unfurled in her brain. She imagined him stepping out of the shorts and peeling off his briefs—if he bothered with any these days. Then he would reach into the shower and turn on the water. Muscles would flex and contract under all that damp, smooth skin. She remembered every ridge and plane of his muscled body. The memory cut right through her, made her weak. She raised her glass and tried to drown the images.

Didn't work.

Oh, yes. She definitely should have stayed on the treadmill longer and stayed away from the wine.

"Bad decision, Eva," she said aloud.

She crossed the room, left the bottle and the glass on her bedside table and grabbed the television remote with both hands. After scanning the entire channel grid, she gave up and tossed the remote onto the bed. Flashes of her bodyguard smoothing a towel over his damp skin kept flickering in her mind. Memories from their past lovemaking whispered through her, making her tremble with need.

"Enough." She did an about-face before she could change her mind and stormed out of her room, straight across the hall and into his room without knocking or stopping or even breathing. The water still raining down in the bathroom didn't halt her either. The door was open so she walked right on in.

Her determined gaze landed on more than six feet of stunning male and then she stopped stone still.

He was still in the shower.

He stood, utterly, gloriously naked beneath the spray of hot water...steam rose around him. He was as beautiful as she remembered. Sleek skin taut over all those perfect muscles. Damp hair clinging to his neck, blue eyes closed. The heat from the shower had him semi-aroused.

As if he'd sensed her presence those pale blue eyes opened. Her heart nearly stopped as he reached to turn off the water, his gaze never leaving hers. He grabbed the towel from the hook next to the shower door and flung it around his hips. His attention focused intently on her, he stepped out of the glass cage and moved toward her like a lion tracking his prey…and she was that prey.

"Are you all right?" His gaze swept over her from head to toe and back as if he'd expected to find a bullet wound or other trauma. The fingers of one hand raked the damp hair from his face. Water trickled down his skin, disappearing into the towel draped low on his lean hips.

For a single second she couldn't move or speak.

"Eva."

The sound of her name on his lips shattered the trance she had slipped into. She closed the short distance between them and stared straight into his eyes. "We should just get this over with so we can move on. Ignoring it is wearing me out."

Those blue eyes narrowed slightly. "How much did you have to drink, Eva?"

"Really?" Her hands went to her hips. "That's all you've got?" She grabbed his face, went up on tiptoe and kissed the hell out of him.

He held absolutely still the first few seconds, his powerful arms hanging at his sides. Her fingers forked into his wet hair and she leaned her body into his damp skin. He made a sound, not quite a growl. Still he didn't give in. She drew her mouth from his, allowed her fingers to trace down his magnificent chest, over mounds of rock-hard muscle. Her gaze followed that incredible path. A smile tugged at her lips when her fingers reached his naval and the swirl of golden hair there.

"Eva, we should talk about this."

"I don't want to talk." She stepped back, peeled off her now damp top and tossed it aside, allowing her breasts to fall free against her chest. Then she shucked the lounge pants, let them hit the floor in a puddle of silky fabric around her feet. Wearing nothing but lacy pink panties, she stepped out of that soft circle and toward him once more.

His gaze roamed down her body, burning her as if he were touching her. The slight hitch in his breath had her heart pounding even harder.

"Are you going to stand there," she asked, "or are you going to man up and do this?"

His jaw hardened and the purely female muscles between her thighs reacted, pulsing with need. Oh, he was angry now.

"You don't want to do this," he growled. "It's the wine."

She laughed. Even the sound of his voice made her nipples burn. "I'm not that naive little virgin you discovered in college. I know exactly what I want and right now it's you. If you think you can handle it, that is."

She sensed the moment he broke. He charged toward her and she lost her breath all over again. He pulled her hard against his body and allowed her to feel just how ready he was beneath that terry cloth. "Don't say I didn't warn you."

"Talk, talk," she accused. He held her so tight she could barely breathe the words.

He yanked the towel from his hips, the friction of it pulling between their bodies making her gasp. He shoved the door shut and trapped her against it. Her legs went around his waist. She pressed down against him, cried out in need.

"Not so fast," he snarled.

His right hand found that place between her thighs that ached so for him. He pushed aside the lace in his way and rubbed until she thought she would die of want and then he slid a finger inside, then another. She whimpered, her eyes closing with the intensity of the pleasure.

"No," he ordered. "Look at me."

She forced her eyes open, read the fury in his. "No more foreplay. Give me what I want. Now," she demanded.

"If we're going to do this we'll do it my way." The pad of his thumb nailed that sensitive spot once more while his fingers plied her body. "I want you looking at me when I make you scream for more."

She dug her heel between the cheeks of his muscled ass and rubbed. He gasped and his eyes drifted shut. "Now who's not looking?" she accused.

His fingers explored more deeply, stretching her, readying her for what was to come. Her breath caught as a ripple of pleasure shot through her. She clamped onto his fingers with those throbbing inner muscles and squeezed. "You keep playing and I'm going to remember I don't really need you to do this," she hissed.

He snatched his fingers away, stared at her, unmoving, his jaw pulsing with more of that fury. Staring into his eyes with matching defiance, she drew one hand from his neck and reached between their bodies. She rubbed that place he refused to assuage and her body tightened with growing desire. Harder, faster, she massaged that sensitive nub until her eyes closed and she moaned with the mounting pleasure. The first waves of orgasm spiraled from the very center of her being. Her body undulated against her hand, wishing it was his wide palm and blunt-tipped fingers.

Suddenly he yanked her hand away and plowed into her. She screamed with the exquisite pain of penetration. He groaned long and loud. For endless moments they didn't move, their bodies joined so completely and yet burning and pulsing for more. He shifted ever so slightly and a full body reaction pulsed through her, taking her over the edge. He stilled, waited, letting her go without him.

Just when she thought her mind and body couldn't take anymore, he started to move. Slow, shallow thrusts, his powerful hips rocking into her. His mouth closed over hers, kissed her, savored her, tasting her lips with his teeth and his tongue and then exploring deeper. His hands tightened on her thighs, pulling her more firmly against him, forcing his thick sex farther inside her.

"Say it," he murmured against her lips.

She bit his jaw.

"Say it," he commanded, nuzzling her cheek with his nose.

"More," she argued.

He thrust harder, deeper. She gasped.

"Say it."

She closed her eyes and lost herself to the new waves building from the inside out, tearing her apart. She arched to meet his powerful thrusts. Cried out with the pleasure-pain of just how deep he was inside her. Orgasm shuddered through her a second time, making her tremble.

He pressed his forehead against the door beside her head and whispered in her ear, "Say it."

She was too weak to argue but somehow she found the strength to cry, "More!"

He pulled her against his chest, flung open the door and carried her to the bed. They came down on the mattress together. One hand went under her bottom, and he lifted her hips to him, opening her wider as he plowed over and over into her. He squeezed her bottom.

She planted her heels on the mattress and met his deep thrusts. "More," she whimpered. Sweat coated their skin, the smell of it comingling with the sweet tang of her orgasms.

With his free hand he stroked her rib cage, trailed his fingers over her, bone by bone, until he grasped her breast. He squeezed, tempted her nipple. She bit her lip to prevent calling his name. She was too weak to fight anymore…too overwhelmed to beg. Her fingers twitched, her toes curled…almost there.

He roared with the orgasm finally overtaking him.

The new waves flowed over her, dragging her into that place of pure sensation a third time while he surrendered to his own.

He groaned a frantic sound as they collapsed together.

Eva closed her eyes against the burn of tears. She should have drunk more of the wine. She should have realized that there was no getting *this* out of the way.

This part of her still belonged to him…

Chapter Nine

Friday, May 11, 8:30 a.m.

Awkward was the word of the day.

Todd opened the fridge and put away the orange juice while plates and forks rattled in the sink. Eva had said exactly six words to him. *Morning*, when she first came into the kitchen. *Yes*, when he'd asked if pancakes would be okay for breakfast. And *I'll get the dishes* when she'd finished eating.

Last night he'd wanted to talk to her about what happened but she'd rushed away so fast he'd barely had time to get his head back down to reality. She'd wriggled free of his arms and left him spent across the bed. When he'd stumbled from the tangled sheets and dragged on his jeans, he'd knocked on her door but she ignored him. He'd heard the water running in the en suite bath. Apparently she couldn't wait to wash him off her skin.

Later he'd wanted to check on her via the security system but the idea had felt completely wrong. Instead, he'd crawled back into his bed and burrowed himself into the scent of her that was all over his sheets, all over his skin. He'd dreamed of their first time together—her first time with any man.

This morning he had awakened wanting more.

She clearly had not.

Their breakfast conversation had consisted of forks scraping against stoneware and coffee mugs settling on the counter. It would be easy to blame what happened on her. She'd come to him after all. But that wouldn't be fair. He was as responsible as she was and no amount of analyzing would change that cold, hard fact.

Dissecting what happened wouldn't alter the bottom line either: he was here to protect her, not take advantage of her vulnerability. Last night she had been vulnerable and he had taken advantage of that vulnerability.

"No work today, right?" he asked, his voice sounding particularly loud after the long minutes of silence. He knew the answer but it was the only conversation opener he could come up with at the moment.

"I volunteer at a walk-in clinic once a

week." She dried her hands. "Today's my day."

He leaned against the counter, keeping at least a half dozen feet between them. "I'll need the address so I can decide on the best route to take and any other relevant info to pass along to Michaels."

Ian Michaels was his backup. Todd kept him apprised of their movements. The worst thing a protective detail could do was fail to report its movements. If communications were compromised, backup would have no idea where to start the search or where to send help.

"Warren Boulevard." She wrapped her arms around her middle and met his gaze for the first time since she clambered out of his bed last night. "It's an old church at the intersection of Warren and Western. Anyone who needs medical attention is welcome. There's no charge. Church donations pay for the needed medical supplies. Several nurses and doctors donate their time. It's important work," she tacked on as if she feared he might debate the day's agenda.

"Maybe I can help, too."

She looked away. "Maybe."

It was highly probable that Robles had

made it a point to learn her routine. "Have you been to the church since last Friday?"

"No." She straightened and tugged at the hem of her blouse.

"Good. Robles might not be aware you volunteer at that location."

Staying aware was key to navigating any area and the level of risk. Anyone looking to commit a crime would always single out a distracted victim over one paying attention.

Her destination was one with which he was familiar and, hopefully, Robles hadn't connected to her. "I'm ready when you are."

"I need to grab my bag."

He watched her walk away. The jeans and gray pullover shirt hugged every sweet curve he had traced with his hands and body last night. He closed his eyes and relived the moment when she interrupted his shower. He'd been done with the shower for a few minutes but he'd stood under the spray of water in hopes it would relieve the tension vibrating in his body. The water hadn't even come close to releasing his tension when she burst in. Watching her strip off her clothes and then stand before him in offering, he'd almost lost it.

She was still as beautiful as he remembered. Every inch of her was perfectly toned yet so damned soft. The first time they were together he'd been terrified that he would hurt her. She'd seemed so tender and fragile. She'd set him straight right from the start. Eva Marie Bowman was strong and tough and damned determined. She and her sister hadn't been shuffled around to foster homes the way he had, but they had experienced their share of tragedy and hard times. Like when their father died, leaving behind a wife who'd never been anything but a homemaker and two young girls who needed a college education. Their mom had worked three minimum-wage jobs to help get them through school. She had died a few years ago while he was still overseas. One of the first things he'd done when he got back to Chicago was take flowers to her grave.

Stella Bowman had liked him. Maybe she'd changed her mind after he left, leaving her daughter's heart broken. Learning to live with that prospect had been almost as hard as leaving Eva in the first place. Even if by some stroke of luck he was able to make amends with Eva, he couldn't change how her mother had gone to her grave feeling about him. Some things couldn't be undone. Yet another of those things was Eva's sister. He wasn't looking forward to running into Lena.

Like most big sisters, she preferred to kick the ass of anyone who hurt her baby sister to talking things over.

"I'm ready," she announced.

He cleared his head and led the way to the garage. At the door he grabbed the keys for the Dodge Charger. He liked that it was black with heavily tinted windows and had an engine made for speed if the need arose.

"We'll take the Charger," he said when she stood at the front of the garage surveying the line of automobiles. He hit the fob and unlocked the doors of the sleek black vehicle that sat third from the right. He'd driven it several times. He felt at home behind the wheel of the Charger more so than the other vehicles.

While she climbed in he set the safe house security system to *away* using his phone. Once he was behind the wheel and had started the engine, the proper garage door automatically opened. As soon as he'd backed out, it closed once more. Five seconds later the garage went into the same *away* lockdown as the house.

For the first few miles he deferred to her decision to keep the silent treatment going. As a soldier in Special Forces he'd learned to wait out the enemies. Hours or days...whatever it took. He'd honed his patience and his ability to remain calm and steady with years of training and operation execution.

But he was no longer a soldier. This was a different world and in this world he was in charge. And he was frustrated and annoyed—mostly at himself.

"About last night—"

"I don't want to talk about last night." She stared out the window at the luxury estates set back amid the lush trees along the road.

Okay, so maybe his strategizing skills where these sorts of things were concerned were a little rusty. Maybe a lot rusty. The past decade he'd satisfied his baser physical needs with one-night stands and no-strings-attached encounters. He hadn't been in a relationship since...

Since he left Eva.

"We should talk about last night anyway." He slowed for a turn. A couple more and they would hit Central Avenue.

"We had sex." She stared straight ahead, her jawline rigid, her hands clutching the armrest as if she feared he intended to rocket into hyper speed. "What's to talk about? It was fine. Good...enough."

"Good enough?" A jolt of outrage joined his mounting frustration. Was she kidding?

The sex had been mind-blowing…fantastic. A second's hesitation nagged at him. No way. She had been thoroughly satisfied. He knew the sounds Eva made when she was enjoying herself. She had enjoyed last night as much as he had.

"That's what I said." She released her grip on the armrest to bend forward and dig around in that enormous leather bag she carried as a purse. He was fairly certain it was the same one she'd carried in college. She called it her good luck bag. It was her last gift from her mother as she entered college. She jammed sunglasses over her eyes and returned her attention forward.

He did the same. The sex had been better than good. She was yanking his chain, trying to tick him off. He got it. Fine.

The truth always came out in the end.

Good Shepherd Church, 11:00 a.m.

"YOU'LL BE AS good as new in a couple of days." Eva smiled at the elderly man whose allergies were giving him a hard time. "Nurse James will give you the meds the doctor prescribed as you leave. Remember to go to the Imaging Center for your appointment for the chest X-ray. Dr. Taggart wants to be sure there's nothing more going on with that nagging cough."

Mr. Hambrick smiled. "Thank you, Eva. You always make my day better."

She gave him a wave as he shuffled off to the checkout area. Her duty here was bittersweet. Seeing all the elderly who had no one else at home or nearby to take care of them or the incredibly poor that had no other means of medical care tugged hard at her heartstrings. On the other hand, knowing that she made a difference in their lives was a soothing balm to her soul.

Certainly made her forget all about her own problems.

As if her mind wanted to remind her that her problems were close, she glanced over at Todd. He was bandaging Rhea Gleason's ankle. She'd managed to cut herself pretty deeply puttering in her flower garden. Eva had inspected Todd's repair work and been duly impressed. With a tetanus shot and an antibiotic just to be sure, Rhea, too, would be fine in a couple of days.

Todd offered his hand to assist Rhea to her feet and she smiled up at him as if he'd whispered a secret to her that only the two of them would ever know. Eva doubted a man as handsome and charming as Todd had ever provided the woman with medical care. Not that Dr. Taggart wasn't charming and quite handsome in his own way—he was. He was also more giving than any doctor she knew besides perhaps Dr. Pierce.

Rhea glanced at Eva and smiled. Todd did the same.

Pretending she hadn't noticed the latter, Eva turned her attention to the sign-in sheet. She called the next patient's name and chatted with the older man as if all were right in her world. Last night should never have happened. She wanted to be glad she'd broken the tension mounting between her and Todd…but she wasn't. The strategy she now recognized as fatally flawed was supposed to prove that Todd Christian wasn't as amazing as she remembered. That the lovemaking skill of the man couldn't possibly be as incredible as the memories. That he would never be able to make this more experienced and mature Eva feel as if her world had tilted on its axis.

You were so wrong, Eva. So, so very wrong.

She'd hoped that at barely nineteen and with no experience that what she remembered was nothing more than blind passion driven by the sweet innocence of first love. Not the case at all. She now fully and undeniably grasped the reason no other kiss, much less any other aspect of lovemaking, ever lived up to his. He was the master. A fantastic lover.

But great sex did not a real relationship make.

Relationship?

She wasn't looking for a relationship.

"Is the old ticker still beating?"

Eva blinked away the distraction, realizing she'd had the diaphragm of her stethoscope against her patient's chest for far longer than it should have taken for her to listen to his heart and lungs.

She smiled and listened a little longer to cover her slip-up, then she removed the tips from her ears. "Sounds as strong as ever, Mr. Fry. Lungs sound clear, too."

Lawrence Fry was seventy and he'd lived in Chicago his whole life. He'd spent most of those years playing a saxophone in various clubs downtown and eventually in the street for donations. He'd told her how the basement of this very church had once been used to hide booze during Prohibition—unbeknownst to the reverend at the time, of course, he always clarified. Fry was one of the most knowledgeable people Eva had ever met when it came to Chicago history, especially the more infamous history.

Like many of their patients he had no family. This free clinic was the only medical care he received. Yet the kind older man never complained. What he did was consistently promise Eva that he intended to play his sax at her wedding. She didn't spoil the moment by informing him there were no plans for a wedding in the foreseeable future.

"That's always good news."

Eva placed the BP cuff around his right arm. "What brings you in today? Are you experiencing any symptoms I need to know about?"

"Actually, I only came so I could see you." He glanced around and leaned forward. "I heard through the grapevine that you're in trouble."

Surprise followed by a trickle of fear made its way into her veins. "You don't need to worry about me, Mr. Fry. I'm doing great, I promise. Where did you hear this?" He kept quiet while she pumped the cuff and took the reading. "One fifteen over seventy. BP looks great."

He took her hand when she reached to undo the cuff. "Word is all over the street that Miguel Robles wants to find you. You aren't safe here or anywhere else, Eva. Don't stay around here so long today. I know this man. He's the worst of the worst. I got mixed up with him and his crew years ago—before he was the big cheese he is now. He's bad, bad news. Watch your back, my friend."

Eva removed the cuff and gave him a nod. "I will. I promise."

He stood and gave her a pat on the shoulder. "I won't take up any more of your time, then. I have a gig over on Harrison Street."

"You be careful, too," she said.

"Always." Mr. Fry winked and ambled on his way.

She watched him go, worry gnawing at her. Nothing he'd said should surprise her, and yet, somehow it did. She kept thinking if she just went on with her life the whole thing would go away.

Not going to be that simple.

Not only was the problem not going away, the news was spreading. Miguel Robles had no choice. He had to save face or risk a revolution against his reign of terror.

The cell strapped to her ankle vibrated. Eva decided to take a break and answer the call in the ladies' room. She moved to the next temporary cubicle to let Betty James know she was taking a break. The exam rooms, so to speak, were made up of all sorts of donated decorative screens from sleek black Asian-inspired wooden ones to metal and fabric shabby chic creations.

Betty gave her a thumbs-up. Eva weaved her way around the makeshift exam rooms and to the entryway of the sanctuary where the restrooms were located. The small entryway was flanked on the left by the women's restroom and on the right by the men's. A double door front entrance was monitored by two uniforms from Chicago's finest. One of the officers, Kelly O'Reilly, waved at her. Every time she worked in this neighborhood he made it a point to stop by and ask her out. Rather than merely stop by today, he and his partner were hanging around. She decided that either Detective Marsh or Todd had warned him about Eva's situation. To avoid questions about her current dilemma or that inevitable awkward moment when she would have to come up with another excuse about not going out with him, she ducked into the restroom before he could catch her.

She'd had more than enough awkwardness today already.

Eva snagged the phone from her ankle and checked the screen. *Lena.* Her heart sped into a run. She hit the screen to return the call and tried to slow the pounding in her chest. When she heard her sister's voice, her knees almost buckled. Thank God. She should have called her already. They lived in the same city and still both of them were bad to let too much time pass between calls and visits.

"Why haven't I heard from you since you moved to this secret location?"

Eva smiled, relieved to hear her sister's snarkiest tone. "Because I've been busy." Flashes of sleek skin and flexing muscles flickered in her brain. Eva pushed them away.

"So, how's it going with Dick?"

Eva laughed. Her sister always did have a way with words. The ability to summarize a situation quickly and eloquently had made her one of Chicago's most beloved reporters. "Things are fine with *Todd*. He's an excellent bodyguard." More of those sensual images and sounds from last night whispered through her mind.

"There was never anything wrong with his body," Lena retorted. "It's his heart where the trouble lies."

"I'm not having this discussion. How's it going in DC?" Why she felt any need whatsoever to defend Todd she would never understand. The idea that her sister's words inspired a glimmer of anger made her want to scream in frustration. But she wouldn't do that either.

"Oh my God."

Those three words told Eva that she was in trouble.

"You slept with him already."

Humiliation and frustration roared through her in equal measures. "I did not sleep with him." It was true. They had sex. There was no sleep involved.

"You never have been a good liar, little sister. You had sex with the man which means that when I get back I have to kick his ass."

Eva burst into full-on laughter. "Kicking his ass will not be necessary. I ended a long dry spell. No big deal. It was just sex."

"Who do you think you're kidding? You ended your dry spell with the jerk who broke your heart when you were just a baby. We need to have a long talk when I get back, sweetie. You have got to start getting out more."

"I was not a baby. I was nineteen." She ignored Lena's other comments. They had been down that "fix her up with this one and then that one" road. Her sister was a great reporter but she totally sucked at matchmaking. "Everyone gets their heart broken, Lena. It's not the end of the world."

She made a rude sound. "It's different when it's your little sister."

"Are you being extra careful?" It was time to change the subject. Eva knew Lena would not let it go unless she ignored further attempts to discuss the matter. Maybe not even then. Persistence was another of her award-winning traits.

"I am. I'm so bored I could take a cooking class. I know this political stuff is super important right now but I'd much rather be back in Chicago doing something that feels more real."

"How about I give you an exclusive when this is over?"

"That's as real as it gets," Lena said softly. "You sure you're okay? You could come stay with me. I'm sure Dick knows what he's doing but I can't help but have reservations."

"He knows what he's doing and I'm being very careful." She stared at herself in the mirror. "I'm at the church clinic today so I really should get back out there."

"I'm doing a story on that soon," Lena warned. "You guys are doing great work. I want the city's uppity-ups to hear about it more often."

"We can always use more donations," Eva admitted.

"You got it. Love you."

"Love you." Eva ended the call and tucked her phone away.

Lena reminded her more of their mother every day. There was just one place where the two had differed immensely. Lena might never forgive Todd for walking away all those years ago when their mother, Stella Bowman, had loved Todd even after he was gone. When he left she had held Eva and promised her she would be fine. She'd also made a prediction or maybe it had been nothing more than wishful thinking. Either way, her mother had been adamant about her conclusion on the matter.

He'll be back one day. You'll see. Todd Christian loves you in a way that can't be ignored.

Tears burned Eva's eyes even now and she swiped them away. "Miss you, Mom."

Eva knew her mother had meant well. She never gave up on anyone she loved. Eva hoped she hadn't spent the last decade unconsciously pushing everyone else away because of what her mother had predicted.

Stella Bowman had been right about one thing. He was back.

But it wasn't for the reason her mother had meant. It was coincidence. And when the tragic events that had aligned to create the chance reunion were no longer a threat to her, he would be gone. Just like before.

Eva drew in a deep breath and pushed out the door. She jumped when her gaze collided with the blue eyes she feared would haunt her dreams for as long as she lived.

"You ready for lunch?" Todd rubbed his lean abdomen. "I'm starving." He hitched his head toward the cop who had a crush on her. "O'Reilly tells me there's a great taco stand next to the Mickey D's across the street. He's even offered to make the food run."

Eva smiled. "Sounds good." She turned to the cop watching Todd like a hawk. "I would love to have lunch with you, Kelly."

He looked from Todd to her and his fierce expression softened. "Text me your order and I'll be back in a snap."

Eva asked Betty and Dr. Taggart if they would like something from the taco stand, and they both declined so she sent her order to Kelly. When he returned she made it a point to chat mostly with him as the three of them ate lunch together.

As she returned to seeing patients she felt Todd watching her. She knew it wasn't right but she was enjoying ignoring her bodyguard.

The idea that he seemed jealous made her far happier than it should.

Sometimes being bad just felt so damned good.

Chapter Ten

6:15 p.m.

Officer O'Reilly and his partner descended the steps at the front of the church with the final two patients of the day. The fondness in Eva's smile as she told Todd how the elderly women who came each week to have their blood pressure checked stirred an unfamiliar longing inside him. The women were sisters, twins no less, and they had lived together since their husbands passed away twelve or so years ago. Both had flirted relentlessly with Todd until he'd escorted them to the door and then they'd turned their gregarious attention to the officers.

Todd hadn't minded. In fact, he hoped he was as healthy as those two when he reached his eighties. He'd been only too happy to take care of the ladies while Eva and the other nurse packed up for the day. While he'd attended to the twins, the screens and portable tables had been stored away in a large supply closet and the remaining medical supplies had been taken away by Dr. Taggart. Eva's team had the set up and the cleanup down to a well-practiced routine.

They would be out of here in the next fifteen minutes. As he surveyed the boulevard that ran in front of the church, he noted the car parked across the street, dark, heavily tinted windows and big, shiny wheels. His warm thoughts of family and all those life-long connections he'd missed, and suddenly found himself wanting, faded with the reality of what was no doubt about to go down.

Trouble.

Easing back into the entryway, he waited until he was out of sight of anyone in the car and then he turned and moved from window to window, checking the streets from every available angle. Thankfully only four of the windows in the main sanctuary were stained glass—the rest were clear, allowing a view of the streets that ran along two sides of the church. Eva had said that donations were slowly but surely replacing all the windows with stained glass to look like what would have originally been in the church. Today, Todd was grateful the renovation was not complete. He spotted at least one other suspicious vehicle.

Damn.

"Christian."

He turned to Rob Gates, the officer working with O'Reilly. Gates hitched his head toward the front entry as O'Reilly joined him. Todd glanced over to Eva and her friend who were finishing the cleanup before joining the two uniforms.

"You saw them, too?"

O'Reilly nodded. "My captain told me to keep an eye out for potential gang members." He nodded toward Eva. "Gates and I have monitored the streets all day. Those lowlifes showed up about two minutes ago. I've already alerted my chain of command that we may have a problem."

Relief rushed through Todd so hard and fast he almost hugged the guy. "You have an ETA for backup?"

"Six, seven minutes." O'Reilly glanced back at the front entrance. "As long as they don't make a move between now and then, we should get out of here with no problems."

But nothing was ever that easy—not when the nastiest of thugs were on the trail of their target.

As if the enemy understood they'd been

made and time was short, the first hail of gunfire shattered the glass in the double front doors and burrowed into the brick walls on either side of the entry.

As O'Reilly and Gates readied to return fire, Todd rushed to Eva and her friend. "Under the pews."

The pews weren't bulletproof by any means but the thick, dense older wood would provide some level of protection, and some was better than none.

Eva grabbed Betty's hand and hurried to do as Todd asked. He took a position at a window facing Warren Boulevard. A quick look verified his worst fears. The bastards were moving in.

"We've got movement," O'Reilly shouted.

Todd kept his head down as he moved back to where the women were hiding. To Eva he said, "They're coming in. We need to find someplace else to hide the two of you."

"The basement," Eva said, fear shining in her eyes.

He shook his head. "We don't want to get pinned down where we can't get out."

"There's a tunnel," Eva explained. "Mr. Fry told me about it."

Todd hesitated again. "What if he's wrong?"

Eva shook her head. "I don't think he is. It's a risk I'm willing to take."

She turned to her friend and the other nurse nodded. "I'm with you."

Eva led the way to the storeroom that had once been a coatroom. A single door on the far side of the room opened to a narrow staircase that plunged nearly straight down. Todd pulled her back. "I go first."

She stepped aside and allowed him to take the first step down. Since he didn't spot a light switch or pull string, he used his cell's flashlight app to see where the hell he was going. "Close the door," he said over his shoulder, "and stay close behind me."

The steps continued downward for about ten feet, ending abruptly at a brick floor. He felt along the wall next to the final step. No switch. Using the flashlight app, he surveyed the small basement and spotted a pull string that led up to an old single bare bulb fixture on a rafter overhead.

He gave the string a yank and a dim glow came to life. Boxes covered in dust lined the far wall. Rows of shelves with books and literature lined another. A couple of tables and several chairs were piled in yet another corner. No windows and no doors.

"Where is this tunnel supposed to be?" Todd looked to Eva.

She shook her head. "I don't know."

"I'll start looking where the books are stored," Betty offered.

Eva headed toward the stack of tables and chairs.

Todd surveyed the bare wall beneath the staircase. No sign of an opening there so he moved on to the boxes. Some of the boxes were fairly heavy, others were so light he wondered if there was anything inside. Then he found the reason for the lighter boxes. Behind them was a small door, maybe two feet by two feet. The door was wood and reminded him of an old-fashioned crawl space door. Both the houses where he'd lived as a curious ten-year-old had doors exactly like this one that led to the area under the house. He and another foster boy had explored the space too many times to recall.

He opened the door. Sure enough, it led to a tunnel that looked to be five or six feet tall, maybe three feet wide and disappeared into the darkness well beyond where his flashlight app would reach. If the exit was sealed off, the find wasn't going to help much. In fact, they could end up trapped like rats.

If there's no exit, you already are.

A deep whoosh resonated overhead. Todd stilled and evaluated the sound. Not gunfire. Not a bomb.

Fire.

"Here!" Todd called, keeping his voice low despite the worry pounding inside him.

Eva and Betty hurried over to his position. "The two of you go first." He pulled the string to extinguish the light. "I'll pull some of the boxes back to the opening to conceal it and then I'll be right behind you."

Footsteps pounded on the stairs. Todd shoved his cell in his back pocket and drew his weapon with one hand and ushered the women into the tunnel with the other. A flashlight beam roved over the room.

"Christian? Eva? You guys down here?"

O'Reilly.

Todd straightened, allowing the officer's flashlight's beam to land on him. "What's going on up there?"

"Molotov cocktails," Gates said. "The old wooden pews are burning like kindling."

"We have to get out of here," O'Reilly urged. "Where're Eva and Betty?"

"This way." Todd ducked into the tunnel. They might die from smoke inhalation if they were trapped in this tunnel, but, hopefully, if it was long enough they could stay away from the danger until help arrived and put out the fire.

Eva and Betty were already at the farthest end of the tunnel.

"There's a ladder," Eva said. She tilted her cell phone flashlight app toward the old wooden ladder. "I don't know if it'll hold us or if the door at the top will open."

Where the ladies stood, the tunnel did a ninety-degree turn, moving upward. The opening was still only three or four feet in circumference but soared upward maybe ten feet.

"Only one way to find out." Todd put his weapon away and grabbed onto the ladder.

He measured the soundness of each rung before putting his full weight onto it. When he reached the door it was much like the one in the basement that had accessed the tunnel, about two feet square. It took some doing to force it open. When he did musty air hit his nostrils. He moved up a couple of rungs and looked around with his cell. The stone piers, the plumbing and ventilation ductwork that snaked around told him it was a crawl space. He climbed out of the hole and looked around a little more. Definitely a crawl space.

"Come on up," he called down to the others.

Eva climbed up the ladder first. Todd helped her out of the tunnel. "Watch your head."

Betty came next, then the two officers.

"This must be the crawl space under the old parsonage," O'Reilly suggested.

"There should be a way out somewhere along the foundation," Todd said, already scanning the outer perimeter. He spotted the small door in the beam of one of the flashlights roving the darkness. "There." He pointed to the north end of the crawl space. "We just have to watch out for the plumbing and the ductwork as we move in that direction."

"And spiders," Betty said.

Eva groaned. "I hate spiders."

"Spiders don't bother me," O'Reilly said. "Snakes, that's what I hate."

Eva and Betty insisted on staying behind the men as they made their way across the cool, musty space. As they crawled toward the exit, the blare of sirens grew closer and closer. Two minutes later they were crawling out into a fenced backyard. What had once been the church parsonage had been turned into apartments. Todd was grateful for the six-foot wood privacy fence that ran between the yard and the church parking lot. The instant he stood he spotted the smoke from the fire at the church.

He swore and shook his head.

O'Reilly took a call as they dusted themselves off. When he put his phone away, he said, "My sergeant says it's all clear. We can head back to the church."

Todd hitched a thumb in the other direction. "I think Eva and I will take another route, just in case they're watching my car."

O'Reilly nodded. "Good idea. They might be laying low, waiting to see if the two of you make it out and planning to follow you away from the commotion at the church if you did. I can have a cruiser pick you up."

Todd shook his head. "One of my colleagues is already en route." He thrust out his hand to the other man. "Thanks for your help."

O'Reilly gave his hand a shake as he glanced at Eva. "Keep her safe. We count on her around here."

Eva and Betty shared a quick hug. Both swiped their eyes. Those bastards had destroyed an important part of this neighborhood—a part all those people who came through the makeshift clinic today depended on. Todd hoped he got the chance to make Miguel Robles pay.

Gates followed his partner's lead and shook Todd's hand next. "Keep your head down, Christian."

"Count on it."

The two officers and Nurse Betty James slipped through the gate next to the house and disappeared. Todd took Eva's hand in his and gestured to the gate at the rear of the yard. "Let's go this way."

EVA WOULD HAVE preferred to go back to the church and assess the damage but she conceded to Todd's judgment. She would find out how badly the church was damaged later. Right now, staying out of sight of those thugs was top priority. Anger roiled inside her at the idea that they had damaged the church to get to her. Now they'd have to find a new place willing to allow them to treat patients from the neighborhood. Every day it was as if her troubles swallowed up more innocent victims. She had to find a way to end this.

As if he sensed her tension, Todd tightened his grip on her hand and urged her forward a little faster. Apparently being lost in thought wasn't conducive to moving quickly. She wondered if he had contacted Ian Michaels again for a ride. She had to give him credit. He was smart not to go back to the car in which they had arrived. Those thugs would be watching. When they'd attacked the church they had known the people inside would have no choice but to find a way out. Made sense that they would eventually end up back at their cars.

But Todd was a step ahead of them.

His strong grip infused her with confidence and warmth, keeping the cold worry and fear at bay. Who would ever have imagined all those years ago when he'd left her brokenhearted that he would one day come back to save her life?

Fate really did have a twisted sense of humor.

They moved along the alleyway between the rows of duplexes and old buildings that reminded her that this part of Chicago represented a century or more of the city's history. The traffic sounds of evening commuters hummed in the air. In another hour it would be dark. Several blocks stood between them and the trouble they'd barely escaped. Eventually they rounded the corner and slowed, walking along Washington Boulevard. Eva recognized the old Fahrney & Sons building. She had an antique medicine bottle from the late nineteenth century with the company name stamped into the glass that had belonged to her grandmother. Her mother had used it as a bud vase. Eva did the same.

Judging by the signs and the scaffolding around the historic building, the piece of Chicago history was finally being renovated. Eva squinted, staring ahead. How much farther did he intend to go on foot? It wasn't that she minded the walk/run pace but she'd been on her feet all day and she was exhausted. Not to mention, she couldn't help but worry that Robles's people would find them somehow.

She tugged on his hand, drawing his determined forward advancement to a halt. "Is your friend coming to pick us up?"

"Yes. We need to keep moving until he gets here."

The sooner they were off the street the happier she would be. The adrenaline had started to recede, leaving her limbs weak. She worked hard not to tremble. No need to show him her fear even if they could have been killed back there.

Betty could have been killed. Their final patients…the two officers Eva had come to consider friends. Her neighbor was dead because of her. A young girl was fighting for her life in the hospital at this very moment because of her.

How foolish she'd been to think that putting herself out in the open and going on with her usual daily activities would somehow make a difference. All she had managed to do was bring the danger to the place she loved most—her work.

"I should go back." She shook her head. "They're never going to stop until they have what they want. Running is doing nothing more than putting off the inevitable."

Todd grabbed her by the shoulders and gently shook her. "So you think giving up is the answer?"

The thought of Mr. Fry or any of the other people she had come to care about being hurt because of her—the way Mrs. Cackowski had been—was more than she could bear. "This can't be fixed by doing nothing but protecting me. Miguel Robles has to be stopped."

"And you believe you can do that?"

The fury in his eyes and in his voice warned that he had lost patience with her on the subject. He'd acquiesced to her demand of going on with her life as usual in an attempt to draw out Robles so the police could catch him. In her defense, she had hoped by baiting him that she would lure him into a mistake. She should have known better. He would simply send more of his minions. He would never risk his own safety.

"I don't know." She closed her eyes and shook her head. "I have to do something."

"You don't let him win," Todd said, his voice softer now. "That's what you do."

Eva steadied herself. "How do I do that without putting everyone I care about in the line of fire?"

And there it was, the million-dollar question no one seemed able to answer.

"We'll talk about this back at the safe house. Our ride is almost here."

She relented, allowed him to usher her forward. He put off answering her question because he couldn't.

The roar of a car engine followed immediately by gunshots jerked Eva's attention to the street. A dark car rocketed toward them.

Todd yanked her toward an old building on their right. He shoved her behind the plywood barrier that blocked off the entrance. Bullets splintered the plywood.

"Keep your head down!" he ordered.

She hunkered down and raced after him. He slammed his body into the sheet of plywood that had been nailed up over the original entrance to the building. More bullets punctured the outer wall of plywood and bit into the brick of the building. She made herself as small as possible and scooted nearer to Todd.

Another slam into the wood and it burst inward. He grabbed her by the hand and ran, clambering over the downed plywood.

With a quick survey of the gutted space, he spotted the staircase and headed that way. The staircase actually looked as if it were standing from memory since not much else appeared to be supporting it. The building had been erected on this piece of property more than a century and a half ago. Hopefully it wouldn't go down so easy. The next staircase looked no better. They rushed up it so fast Eva wondered if their feet even touched the treads.

No sooner than they reached the second floor, the sound of running footfalls echoed from the first floor.

With no police around, the thugs had apparently decided to give chase beyond the protection of their cars.

Just her luck.

Todd stalled.

Eva plowed into his back. Rather than ask why he'd stopped moving she stared at the place where the next staircase should have been.

It was gone.

They were trapped.

Todd checked his cell. He surveyed their situation once more as he shoved the phone into his back pocket. Then his hand tightened on hers once more and he said, "This way."

Shouting downstairs warned that the men were closing in on the second staircase.

She and Todd reached the backside of the building. He moved toward a large hole that might have once been a couple of windows. It wasn't until they skidded to a stop at that hole that she saw the slide-like setup going from this floor down to the huge construction Dumpster on the ground.

"I'm going down first," he said as he slung one leg onto the slide. "Grab on to my waist and stay tight against me so I can cushion your landing."

There was no time to question the proposed exit. She grabbed on to his lean waist and held on tight.

Her stomach shot into her throat as they whooshed downward. They landed on a pile of construction debris.

Todd grunted.

Before she could ask him if he was okay, he forced her up and over the side of the Dumpster. He was right behind her.

A dark sedan rolled toward them.

Eva stalled, her heart dropping to her feet in a sharp free-fall.

Todd pulled her against him and sprinted the last few yards—toward the car. He yanked the rear door open and they landed on the back seat with the car still rolling.

"Go! Go! Go!" Todd shouted.

The car spun forward. Todd jerked the door shut and ushered Eva onto the floorboard.

Bullets pinged against the metal exterior.

Todd was suddenly on top of her and they were speeding away.

Chapter Eleven

Colby Safe House, 9:30 p.m.

Eva set the hair dryer aside and reached for the hairbrush. She dragged it through her hair, her thoughts far from the task. The fire gutted the church. She felt sick at the news. Dr. Taggart had sent her a text assuring her he'd spoken to the reverend and there was insurance which would eventually do the repairs, but there was no way to know how long that would take.

At least no one else had died.

Ian Michaels had explained that two other Colby Agency investigators were working on the case. Their efforts were being coordinated with Chicago PD. Eva appreciated the lengths to which they were willing to go. She hoped they were more successful than the local police had been so far.

Not fair, Eva. The police couldn't stop Robles if they had no evidence against him.

She braced her hands on the counter and stared at her reflection in the mirror. Her resolve was faltering, her determination running on empty. The past two days had been some of the hardest of her life. As exhausted and keyed up as she was, she wouldn't be going anywhere near the wine tonight. Not after how she'd allowed herself to go completely over the edge last night.

She turned away from the sad, uncertain woman in the mirror and padded back into the bedroom. A single functional brain cell reminded her that she should eat, but food was the furthest thought from her mind. Her mood fluctuated between defeated and furious. In her whole life she had never felt more helpless…more uncertain of the future. To make matters worse, she had lost her cell phone in the fray of today's frantic escape. Tomorrow she'd have to pick up a new phone and deal with transferring her contacts and other content. Eva sighed. Sometimes it felt like more of her life was available as data rather than as a real life. When had her existence become so dependent on notifications and alerts coming from a tiny object scarcely larger than a credit card?

She wandered to the door. Todd had promised they would talk about her concerns later. It was later and he'd avoided a face-to-face with her since they'd agreed that showers would do them both a world of good. He'd headed to his room and she'd headed to hers. Scarcely five feet of carpeted hallway stood between the two doors. She should just go over there, knock on the door and demand to know if he was ready to talk, or simply tell him she was heading downstairs and would be waiting for him so they could have the promised discussion.

Dredging up her battered wherewithal, she opened her door and took the three strides to his door. She curled her fingers into a fist and reached up to knock and his door abruptly opened.

He blinked, stared at her and then his lips parted as if he intended to speak, but no words made it past the tip of his tongue.

She took a breath and prepared to launch the first question but her attention stalled on his bare chest. It wasn't like she hadn't seen his chest hundreds of times. Well, maybe not hundreds but at least one hundred. His skin was damp as if he'd hastily scrubbed the towel over that sleek terrain. A drop of water slipped down his lean, rippled abdomen. She jerked her gaze upward as his torso widened into the broad shoulders where she'd lain her head dozens of times, moving on to the strong, muscled arms that had held her close on so many occasions.

Her attention whipped back to his right shoulder. A wad of gauze stained with crimson was stuck there. "What happened?"

He grinned, the expression a little lopsided. "I guess a nail or something from the construction heap snagged me. I can't reach it with both hands to do the repair."

Eva frowned. She remembered his shirt being torn in a couple of places. Hers had been as well but she'd walked away with nothing but a few sore places that would likely turn into bruises. "Let me have a look."

He moved into the hall, stepping away from her as he did. "I'll get the first aid kit then you can take care of it. I'll be right back."

He hurried down the stairs before she could do the smart thing and suggest they take care of his wound in the kitchen—far away from sheets still perfumed with their lovemaking. Instead, Eva stared after him for a few moments, then she hugged her arms around herself and entered his room. She felt somehow cold and too warm at the same time. No one had been seriously injured or killed today, she was grateful. Still, the potential...the what-ifs throbbed in her skull. Betty or Dr. Taggart could have been hurt. Officers O'Reilly and Gates—Todd could have been killed trying to protect her and Betty. If not for the quick thinking of Todd and O'Reilly, the day may have ended far more tragically.

How in the world did she fix this and stay alive?

She needed some plan of action. Todd's military training and work with the Colby Agency made him the better choice at figuring out a doable plan of action. Her problem was getting him to go there. He would like nothing better than for her to stay in hiding until this was over. That route wasn't feasible. Deep down he had to know this. Dr. Pierce surely grasped that fact as well—which brought up a whole other issue. How could she expect Pierce to hold her position without a reasonable return-to-work date?

She couldn't.

Pushing the troubling thoughts aside she surveyed Todd's bedroom. She hadn't gotten much of a look at it last night. Flashes of bare skin and flexing muscles filtered through her weary mind along with whispered words and soft sounds. How had she ever believed for even a minute that any other man could make her feel the way he did? There had been others, a few. Not one had been able to touch that place inside her that only Todd Christian had reached.

Again she cleared her head and focused on the mundane details. The layout of his room was much like her own, a large space with elegant furnishings. The closet door was open, as was the door to the en suite bath. He'd tossed a T-shirt on the bed.

Her throat tightened as her gaze moved over the rumpled bed.

Closet. Stick to the far less dangerous spaces. She shifted her gaze to the closet. His duffel bag had been delivered here which made her wonder again why she'd ended up with a new wardrobe. Maybe it was the privacy issue of going through her things. On the other hand, it might simply be the best way to ensure nothing of sentimental value that belonged to her was damaged in all this running for their lives.

She ran her fingers along the shirts and tees that hung in a neat row in the closet. Jeans and a pair of black trousers were efficiently folded and placed on a shelf. A pair of leather loafers sat on the floor beneath the hanging shirts. The military had made him a little neater than she recalled.

With a deep sigh that made her heart uncomfortable, she turned away from his clothes and wandered to the door of the bathroom. A bottle of aftershave sat on the counter alongside a comb and a razor. The aftershave was the same one he'd always worn. Subtle hints of leather and sandalwood with the tiniest trace of citrus. She didn't have to look in the shower to know there would be a matching bodywash. The gentle fragrance of the toiletries he chose was so understated that his own natural scent was by far the more distinct.

His clothes, his car, even the apartment where he'd lived before had been modest, understated. The man himself had always been what stood out. How was it that a man so unpretentious and kind could have stolen her heart and then walked away without looking back? So many times she had asked herself that question. Had he found someone new? Had he grown bored with her? Had she done or said something that pushed him away? Yet, deep down she somehow understood that his decision was not her fault. He'd left for reasons she did not comprehend. But she hadn't come to that conclusion overnight. It had taken months, perhaps even years to realize that she'd done nothing wrong. Todd Christian had decided to walk away.

End of story.

"Sorry. It took me a minute."

Eva turned to face him. She'd intended to tell him to have a seat so she could look at his shoulder. Instead, she blurted, "Why did you leave without so much as saying goodbye?"

His fingers tightened on the first aid case. Eva vaguely wondered if it would suddenly crack and fall to pieces as her heart had all those years ago.

"What?"

His apparent confusion frustrated her. "You just left one day and never came back." She shrugged. "You didn't say a word or leave a note. I never heard from you again. I'm asking you why. Why did you do something so callous?"

He gave a single, small nod of his head. "Fair question." He waved the first aid case toward the bathroom. "I'll give you the best answer I know how while you work."

Surprised that he'd caved to her demand so easily, she followed him into the bathroom where he closed the toilet lid and sat down. He placed the case on the counter and stared at the wall he faced.

Eva decided to give him a moment while she surveyed the available medical supplies. The case offered the usual home first aid kit supplies with a few extras. In addition to the usual items, bandages, gauze, antibacterial and antihistamine creams, and antiseptic wipes, there were suture kits and butterfly bandages, tweezers and even a small scalpel.

"There's no lidocaine." Not a good thing in her opinion. "You're going to feel this."

"Just do it. I've endured worse."

His words had her wondering about the small scar on his cheek and the others on his back, but she decided not to distract him from the question she'd already asked. She washed her hands and walked around one muscled leg to reach his shoulder. The position put her square in the *V* of his muscular thighs. Her body reacted with a familiar twinge between her own thighs. How would it be possible not to react to the half-naked, good-looking man who'd saved her life? Particularly one who still owned a considerable chunk of real estate in the vicinity of her heart?

He will never know that sad truth.

Putting those reactions on ignore, she slowly pulled the gauze free of his skin and then tossed it into the sink. The gash was not too deep, not so wide, but the sides were not going to stay together without some assistance. She considered the butterfly bandages but she doubted those would hold the next time they were in a desperate situation. A few stitches would do the trick.

"I cleaned it with bottled water and a little bleach since I didn't have any betadine handy. I didn't see any debris that shouldn't be there, like splinters."

"Good." Eva threaded the eye of the needle with the sutures. She pulled the wound together, getting it as close to pre-gash condition as possible. "You were going to answer my question." She located the spot where she wanted to begin and inserted the needle through the skin.

He grimaced, made a small sound, not quite a grunt.

"Sorry." She secured the first suture and began working back toward the edge. In, out, pull, repeat.

She'd almost reached the final suture when he finally spoke. "I shouldn't have left the way I did. I was a coward."

Of all the answers she'd expected him to give, that was not one of them. Rather than say so, she kept her lips in a tight line and finished sealing the wound with a precise knot to keep the sutures just snug enough to aid in healing without injuring the skin further.

"I spent most of the first eighteen years of my life being tossed from foster home to foster home." He exhaled a big breath. "You were the first person I ever really wanted to please—beyond physically, I mean."

Struggling to keep her hand steady, she set the suturing tools aside and reached for antibacterial ointment. She applied a thin layer and then prepared a proper bandage with gauze and tape. All the while her heart pounded at his confession.

"I'd never wanted to make anyone happy like that before. I wanted to give you everything…to be everything you wanted."

Anger sparked. "I never wanted everything."

He shook his head. "Even if you'd said so at the time, it wouldn't have changed what I wanted."

Her work complete, Eva closed her eyes and dropped her hands to her sides. When she could say the words without her voice trembling, she opened her eyes and asked, "What changed your mind?"

"One morning I woke up and you were still sleeping." He turned his face up to hers, his blue eyes begging for forgiveness or understanding. "I stared at you for so long, wondering how I would ever be the kind of man you deserved. I had no pattern to follow. How could I be the kind of man you could depend on when I wasn't sure I could depend on myself?"

On some level she wanted to understand his reasoning, but she couldn't. How selfless of him to throw away all her hopes and dreams to ensure he didn't hurt her. Ha! Outrage flamed deep in her soul, raging instantly out of control. "Wow. You really gave up everything to save me, didn't you? And all this time I thought you were a selfish ass for leaving without a word."

He looked away. "I needed to grow up. To learn to trust myself before I could let you put all your trust in me."

Incredible. "What a shame your timing was about six months too late." Eva moved away from him, threw the supplies back into the case. "I'm so glad we had this talk. I totally get why you left now."

He pushed to his feet, moved in on her and stared at her in the mirror when she wouldn't look at him. "It was the hardest thing I've ever done. Leaving you tore me apart."

Eva glared back at him. It would be so easy to believe him. To fall back into loving him, just like before. "So you went off to the military and let them make a man out of you, is that it?"

"Pretty much. That and time."

"Well, I'm glad I was a part of your learning curve." She scooted away from him and headed for the door.

She was halfway across his room before he caught up with her. His fingers curled around her arm and pulled her to a stop.

"What?" she demanded. The sooner she was out of here, the better. She should never have gone down that path with him. Now he knew that a part of her still pined after him. How pathetic was that?

TODD HAD MADE a mess of his explanation. Every damned word had come out wrong. Rather than explain himself, he'd excused himself. Not what he'd intended. "I was wrong. What I did was wrong. There is no excuse."

She glared up at him and the hurt in her beautiful green eyes made his chest ache. "Glad you've seen the error of your ways. Now, if you'll excuse me, I'd like to get some sleep."

He released her but he wasn't ready to let her go. "I thought you wanted to talk about a plan for getting Robles."

She hesitated at the door. "I already know what to do." She turned to face him. "I tell the police I'd like to help set a trap for him.

The sooner the better. It works in the movies all the time."

He moved toward her, choosing his words carefully. "This isn't the movies. Real life rarely works that way."

"I've run out of ideas and I refuse to be a party to another day like this one or like yesterday. I want to finish this thing I set in motion when I killed that son of a bitch."

When she would have turned to walk out the door, he reached over her and closed it. "I won't let you do that."

She turned and glared up at him. "You can't stop me."

He moved in a step nearer, trapping her against the door. "Watch me." He cupped her face in his hands and leaned in close. "I will not let you do this."

She tried to back away, but the door stopped her. "Is this your way of making up for the past? You'll keep me safe and assuage your guilt?" She shook her head. "Like you said, this isn't the movies, this is real life. You can't repair the heart you shattered all those years ago by being the hero today. I can't forgive you for what you did, Todd. If that's what you're expecting, you've overestimated your worthiness."

Her words were like daggers twisting in his chest. "You hate me, is that it?"

She blinked. "Maybe."

"You hate me so much—" he braced his forearms on the door and leaned into her, putting his face right up to hers "—that you came over and over in my arms last night."

She stared at his lips a moment and he longed to taste her. "That was sex," she argued. "Nothing more."

"Sex?" He traced her cheek with his nose. "Just sex?"

"Yes."

The feel of her lips moving against his jaw made him so damn hard he could barely breathe. "Then you won't mind if we do it again, just to be sure it was only physical." He brought his mouth around to hers. She gasped. "It doesn't mean anything." He nipped her bottom lip. "Just sex."

She stilled, lifted her eyes to his. "I've already experienced all your parlor tricks, Christian. I doubt you can show me anything new. I'd suggest you save your strength for helping me take down Miguel Robles."

Parlor tricks, eh? "Give me a minute to change your mind."

When she would have argued, he dropped to his knees. He reached for the waistband of her lounge pants and slid the soft fabric down her thighs, letting them fall to the floor. No panties. His body reacted with a rush of need that rocked him and had his cock pushing against his fly. He kissed her belly button, traced over her belly with his tongue. She pressed against the closed door as if to escape the exquisite torture, her hands braced on either side of it.

He lifted her right leg and settled the crook of her knee onto his left shoulder. Let her try to escape. He was only getting started. She gasped as he bent his head toward the tender flesh between her thighs. He kissed every part of her, slid his tongue along that delicious channel. She whimpered softly. Still she kept her hands plastered against the door. He delved deeper, using his mouth to draw on that place that caused her to cry out. He dipped a finger inside her, savored the moist, sweet heat and then tested her with another.

Her fingers suddenly dove into his hair as if to hold him back. He stilled and then she gasped, surrendering as her body started an instinctive, rhythmic undulating. He used his fingers, his tongue, his lips to explore all of her most intimate places, to bring her to orgasm. She cried out with the pleasure. He kissed her belly, moved up her torso, letting her leg slip down, her foot land on the floor, as he tasted his way to her breasts. He wanted to memorize every inch of her. He savored her breasts with his mouth while he used his fingers to draw her toward climax again. Hot, firm nipples peaked for his attention while those sweet feminine muscles tightened around him. He pressed the pad of his thumb harder against her clitoris. She fought to restrain her cries, but he could feel how hard and fast she was coming undone all over again. Her fingers found his fly and struggled to unfasten his pants. She managed to push his jeans down, releasing his aching cock, but he refused to give her what she wanted just yet. She whimpered with need, rubbed him wantonly with her hands.

When she reached that edge...so very close to exploding with pleasure yet again, he turned her around so fast she lost her breath. He pushed between her thighs, reached around her small waist with one hand and down to that wet, pulsing place to guide himself into her. She screamed with pleasure as he pushed deep inside her. He kept one hand focused on that hot, pulsing nub and the other on her breasts, kneading each one in turn, tweaking those perfect hard nipples. He pressed her against the door as he thrust in and out. This position took him so deep, stretching her to the very limits and she cried out for more.

One more hard, deep thrust and they came together.

With her back pressed against his chest and his cock deep inside her, he carried her to the bed. When he would have pulled out of her, she arched her bottom, keeping him deep inside that hot, wet place as they started that sweet, slow rocking motion all over again.

Chapter Twelve

Saturday, May 12, 8:00 a.m.

Eva couldn't blame the wine this time.

Todd had broken through all her defenses, lowered every wall she had so carefully erected over the past ten years to protect her battered heart. Bared her every vulnerability, revealed her rawest emotions. By the time they'd both collapsed, utterly exhausted, she couldn't have argued about the best course of action to take against Robles any more than she could have crossed the hall to her own bed.

When she'd awakened, he'd already been downstairs. She was glad. She'd needed the past forty minutes to gather her scattered composure. This morning she intended to get straight down to business. She had a life she wanted to get back to. She wanted this ugly situation cleared up before her sister returned to Chicago. She needed distance from Todd before she lost her heart and soul to him all over again.

A quick shower had washed his scent from her skin but nothing could scrub those hours from her memory or the sweet ache from her muscles. The way he touched her, as if he knew every part of her and understood how to reach her deepest desires. He had explored every inch of her and she had done the same, relearning his lean, muscled body. Tasting him, touching places that had haunted her dreams for so very long.

She wasn't the only one who had been pushed beyond all carefully lain boundaries—she had given as good as she got. She had made him groan with need, watched his fingers clench in the sheets, made him beg for more. He'd whispered her name over and over. They'd climaxed together so many times, she felt weak with pleasure even now, overwhelmed with the need to touch him again and again.

Todd Christian was a drug she would never be able to resist.

With that undeniable knowledge tucked away for later contemplation, she left her room and headed for the stairs. The smell of bacon lingered in the air as she descended the staircase. Her stomach rumbled and she suddenly realized she was starving. More often than not she grabbed a cup of yogurt and a piece of fruit for breakfast. After what she'd been through the past few days, she had every right to splurge with a self-indulgent breakfast.

Todd looked up from the stove as she walked into the room. His grin was sexy as hell and made her heart skip a beat. "Good morning."

"Good morning." She headed straight for the coffee pot and poured a cup. The rich aroma had her immediately lifting the cup to her lips. Bold flavor burst on her taste buds and she made a satisfied sound. "So good."

"I hope you still like pancakes."

She turned to him, the warm cup cradled in both hands. "The ones with nuts and whole wheat flour?"

"That's the ones." He paddled three pancakes onto a plate and slathered a pat of butter on top, then piled on the bacon. "Since we discovered this recipe, I've never made pancakes any other way."

She wondered how many other women he'd made them for after a long night of hot sex. *None of your business, Eva.*

She claimed a stool while he prepared his

own plate and poured them both a glass of orange juice. This could be her last breakfast. After what happened yesterday, it was clear Robles didn't intend to back off. She should claim whatever pleasure available. She blocked more images from last night and focused on the aromas making her mouth water this morning.

"Wow." She dismissed the foolish and wholly unfounded worry about other women. "I can't believe you remembered how I like my pancakes."

He reached around her and poured on the syrup. "You're the only person I've ever made pancakes for."

She smiled, ridiculously pleased by his comment as she lifted a forkful of deliciousness to her mouth. Another of those happy moans vibrated inside her. The pancakes were so good. She grabbed a slice of crisp bacon and devoured it before reaching for her juice. "I might just die right here."

He laughed. "Then I'd have to face the wrath of Lena."

Eva put her hand over her mouth to prevent spewing orange juice. "True."

He fell silent for a minute but she sensed he had more to say. Had he learned something new about her case?

She set her fork aside and turned to him. "Did something else happen?" *Please, don't let anyone else be dead because of her.*

Realization dawned in his eyes. "No. No, nothing else has happened." He dropped his fork onto the counter. "I was thinking about your mom and how sorry I am that I didn't get a chance to apologize to her for what happened. She must have hated me after…after I left."

Eva picked at her pancakes. "No. She didn't hate you. She adored you."

Surprise replaced the sadness she'd seen in his expression only moments ago. "Are you sure about that? I mean, Lena made it pretty clear how she felt."

She would not—could not—tell him all her mother said. "Lena is Lena, but trust me when I say my mother adored you until the day she died."

"Thank you." He reached out and gave her hand a squeeze. "I appreciate you telling me."

Eva blinked, then looked again. The shine of emotion was heavy in his eyes. She turned away. Maybe slaving over a hot stove had made him teary-eyed. "It's true. She loved you." She clamped her teeth together, could have bitten off her tongue. She hadn't meant to use the *L* word, though her mother made her feelings about Todd clear on numerous occasions. He was the son she never had.

He drew his hand from hers as if her blurted words had stung him almost as badly as they had her. It was definitely time for a change of subject.

"So you joined the army." Her voice sounded too high-pitched and she cursed herself for even speaking again.

He shifted his attention back to his plate. "I did. My specialty was communications at first." He shrugged. "Apparently there was a shortage in the field since I expected to be an eleven bang-bang—an infantry soldier."

"You were an officer?" He'd just graduated with his degree in science. For hours on end he would talk about how he wanted to be a teacher. A few teachers were the only people who had ever made him feel as if he could be more than what he'd come from.

"No." He shook his head. "They offered me the opportunity but I didn't want to be an officer. I wanted to do what all the other enlisted soldiers had to do."

"Really?" Surprised, she munched on another slice of bacon. "Did you travel the world?"

"Not so much at first." He reached for his coffee. "A couple years after my enlistment,

I was recruited by Special Forces. Everything changed then."

She laughed in hopes of lightening the moment. "I suppose you went on all sorts of exciting top secret assignments in Special Forces."

"Now and then." He poked at the pile of pancakes on his plate.

"Is that where you got the scars?" She touched her cheek in the same spot where the scar was on his. It was such a small one, but there were several larger ones on his back. Not a single one detracted from his good looks. She bit her lips together for fear she'd throw in that part, too.

"Shrapnel. I was one of the lucky ones."

Shrapnel meant a blast...a bomb. He could have been killed—probably numerous times. The realization made her angry. Why had he worked so hard in college to achieve his degree—not to mention he'd been accepted into a master's program—just to throw it all away? "What happened to the teaching career you talked about?"

He stared at his plate once more and lifted one shoulder in a halfhearted shrug. "I guess that was another one of those things I figured I didn't deserve."

Why had she never once noticed that deep-seated worry about his self-worth when they were together? Had she loved him so much that she couldn't see the pain? The idea made her sad. But she'd been so young...

"What about Kevin? Have the two of you kept in touch?"

He smiled, and the beauty of it took her breath away. "He graduated law school last year. He just got married. I was his best man."

"That's great." How many times had she planned *their* wedding before he ran away?

The rest of the meal was eaten in silence. Eva had said more than enough. So had he. She couldn't decide which was worse: all the things she'd told him, or the things she allowed herself to do with him.

Or maybe it was all that he hadn't told her when it mattered most.

With every fiber of her being she understood one thing with complete certainty: when this was over—assuming she survived—she would be heartbroken once more because he would leave again.

Some people just never learned.

EVA INSISTED ON cleaning up. Todd tried to help but she shooed him away. "You cooked. I'll clean."

He held up his hands and backed away from the sink. "Have it your way."

A break would do him good. He'd been on edge all morning. Well, no, maybe it started last night after hours of incredible lovemaking. He'd lain awake for hours just watching her sleep. No one had ever made him feel as important and as helpless at the same time as Eva did. She made him yearn to be more… to give her more.

"I'll be in the office." He hitched a thumb toward the hall. "We can have that talk about Robles and where we go from here when you're done."

Her eyebrows reared upward. "Seriously? You're not going to find a way to put me off again or to change the subject?"

His last attempt to distract her had taken an unexpected turn and he'd ended up on his knees. Who was he kidding? He'd dreamed of savoring all of Eva from the moment he saw her again. For years he'd kept thoughts of her—the memories—locked away in a place in his heart that refused to let go of her. He'd ignored those memories for years, unable to touch them. Then he'd returned to Chicago and he'd seen her by complete accident for the first time in more than eight years. She hadn't seen him so he'd followed her and his entire being had ached with the need to touch her…to know her again. If he was honest with himself, he would admit that he'd been trying hard to work up the nerve to talk to her for more than a year. He'd followed her enough times that he felt like a stalker.

Gotta get your head straight, man.

Right now he had a job to do. One of the most important of his life; he had to keep Eva safe. As he walked toward the office he called Michaels to see if there was any news on the agency's investigation into Robles.

Michaels said, "I was about to call you."

Not a good sign. "I take it you've found someone willing to talk."

The agency had concentrated on finding evidence of the gang leader's crimes while Todd focused on protecting Eva. Victoria wanted to do what the police had not been able to—find someone willing to testify against Robles.

"We have and that source warned that Robles is about to make a direct move against Eva. Since her sister is her only family, I've contacted a colleague in DC to put eyes on her. That's a considerable reach for Robles, but at this point he's likely feeling desperate to avenge his brother. More than a week has passed and he hasn't managed to follow through with his declaration of vengeance."

"Never a good thing for the minions to see." Todd agreed completely. Robles was no doubt damned desperate by now. He'd probably exterminated every member of his gang who'd failed to bring Eva to him.

"If our source will testify against Robles, we may have a starting place for Gang Intelligence to build a real, prosecutable case. Until now, they haven't had a source willing to speak out against Robles. But his credibility is in question now. Every day he fails to honor his brother, his followers grow more restless."

"Maybe the world will get lucky and they'll start killing each other." As crazy as it sounded, it happened. Someone inside could decide Robles was too weak to continue to be their leader. It was a long shot but a guy could hope.

"Until then we keep Eva and her sister safe and we continue pursuing potential sources."

They discussed the various avenues for further infiltrating the True Disciples as well as Victoria's urgent requests to her higher-level resources. If anyone could find a way to Robles, it was Victoria.

"Thanks for the update." Todd was grateful for every step that brought them closer to ending the danger to Eva. "Keep us posted."

He ended the call and put his cell away. Now if he could convince Eva to be patient a little longer—

"What update?"

He did an about-face and produced a smile. Eva was the only person who had ever been able to sneak up on him. He'd decided back when they were together that it was because she was such a part of him. They were one. His senses wouldn't alert him to her presence any more than they would warn his right arm that his left was nearby. They began and ended together.

Evidently his instincts hadn't realized that wasn't the case anymore.

Whispers and glimpses of last night's urgent lovemaking echoed through him. Maybe in some ways it was still the same, which was a blessing and a curse at the same time.

"We have a source who may be willing to testify against Robles."

Her eyes widened with anticipation. "Would that be enough to get him off the streets?"

"Depending on what information he has and how much of it he can back up, it's possible. If we're really lucky charges could be brought and the judge would deny bail." He resisted the urge to reach out and touch her in reassurance. "It's a starting place."

He decided not to tell her about Michaels's other concerns. Michaels was on it. Lena would have protection ASAP if it wasn't in place already.

Eva moved into the room, her arms folded over her breasts in a protective manner. "Do you believe he can be stopped this way? I don't understand why that hasn't happened already if it's so simple."

His hands twitched with the need to pull her close and hold her as he explained what Michaels had told him. "He's swiftly losing credibility. Power and fear are the two main ingredients of a dictator's reign and that's what gang leaders like Robles are. He has hundreds of followers and they do as he tells them for various reasons. Some idolize him. Others are too afraid to do otherwise. The life—meaning their membership in the gang—is all they've ever known."

"Afraid?" She frowned. "Why would cold-hearted killers be afraid of anything?"

"Those who have second-guessed the life are in too deep to turn back now. Leaving isn't an option. They'd be hunted and killed as would the people they care about. For others, they might be fearless when it comes to fighting, maiming and murdering, but they're terrified of not having the unity they find in the gang. In some cases, it's the only family they've ever known. If their leader fails, someone worse or someone who might not want them could take over. For those guys, protecting the life is all that matters."

"Either way it seems like the empire Robles has built might be on shaky ground." Hope glimmered in her eyes.

Todd was grateful the news had given her something to hang on to. Maybe it would be enough to keep her smart about how to proceed. "Every day that you're breathing, his credibility weakens. Someone else could step up and go for a takeover."

"How can I help make it happen faster?" She turned her palms up in question. "I could go on the news. Speak out about what a coward he is."

Todd managed a stiff laugh that came out more like a cough. "I think we'll hold off on that avenue for a bit."

"This is good news, though." She hugged herself again, rubbed her hands up and down her arms as if she were chilled. "I should call Lena. Let her know I'm okay. We haven't spoken since early yesterday." A frown furrowed her brow. "She hasn't answered that text I sent from your phone last night letting her know I was okay after what happened at the church."

He dug his phone from his back pocket and offered it to her. "She hasn't. Why don't you give her a call? I'll have a new phone brought to you, if you'd like."

She accepted the phone. "I'm guessing that means we're staying in today."

Before he could answer, his cell rang. Eva jumped and almost dropped it.

She passed it to him. "Geez, that scared the hell out of me."

Todd didn't recognize the local number. "Christian."

"Christian, this is Detective Marsh. We have a problem."

"I'm listening." Todd moved to a desk and awakened a computer monitor just to put some distance between him and Eva without being too obvious about it.

"Someone broke into Lena Bowman's townhouse last night. They tore the place apart and left a vic in the bedroom. We're going to need Eva to come over here and make an identification."

Todd's heart stumbled. "Can you give me a few more specific details?"

"The vic is female. We can't be sure

whether or not it's her sister. The general height and weight, hair color are right, but there's too much facial damage to be certain."

Fear snaked around his chest and tightened like a vise. Lena was out of town. Couldn't be her. Still, his gut churned with worry. "We'll be right there."

With great effort he slid the phone back into his pocket without allowing his hand to shake. The worry and no small amount of fear crushed against him. "We have to go to Lena's apartment." He started for the door, taking Eva by the arm and pulling her along as he went.

"Why?"

He kept his gaze forward. Making eye contact right now he feared would show her what he didn't want her to see—not yet anyway. "Someone broke in and ransacked the place."

"Okay," she said, the word thin.

He wouldn't mention the rest until they were there. Having her get hysterical while he needed to watch for a tail could get them both in trouble.

As if she sensed there was something more he wasn't saying, she didn't ask anything else as they loaded into the black Camaro. The next forty-five minutes were some of the longest in his life. Eva tried four times to call her sister. Each time the call went to voice mail. His tension rocketed higher. Thankfully, Eva didn't start asking questions.

By the time they reached Lena's townhouse on East Elm Street, Eva was quietly falling apart piece by piece. Her hands were trembling and she stared out the window. He roared right up to the police perimeter and two uniforms shouted orders for him to move and that this was a crime scene. Like the strands of yellow tape weren't sufficient evidence it was a crime scene. Pedestrians and neighbors stood on the sidewalk across the street and behind the tape. A couple of news vans were already on the scene but they had been held back a full block.

"Detective Marsh is expecting us," Todd said to the officer who marched up to him.

A sharp whistle sounded from the townhouse steps. Marsh motioned at the officer. "Let 'em through."

Todd put his hand to Eva's back and guided her to the steps. Her shoulders were square and her stride was firm, but he felt her body trembling. Marsh waited on the sidewalk to walk up with them. Lena's place was the upper of the two units.

"I'm sorry I had to call you over here,

Ms. Bowman," Marsh said as they walked through the front door.

"Can you give us a minute?" Todd asked when they stood in the entry hall with the front door closed, blocking out the prying eyes on the street.

Marsh gave a knowing nod. "Sure. I'll wait in the living room."

Todd turned to Eva and he would give anything in the world not to have to tell her the part he'd been holding back.

As if she suddenly understood what he was about to say, Eva shook her head. "She isn't here. Lena's in DC. You know that."

"I know." He wished his heart would stop pounding so hard and that his hands would stop their damned shaking. "There's a woman, Eva. She was murdered in the bedroom."

Eva fought to keep her expression clean of emotion but her lips trembled and she made this hiccupping sound that ripped his thundering heart right out of his chest even as she shook her head adamantly once more. "She's not here."

He tried to take her hand but she dodged the move. "You're right," he said, the two words uttered out of sheer desperation. "Marsh thought maybe it was one of her neighbors.

He hoped you might be able to help them with the identification."

More of those painful sounds wrenched from her throat. "Liar."

"Come on." He closed his hand around hers before she could snatch it away from him this time. "Let's do what we can to help Marsh and then we can get out of here."

She nodded, the movement jerky.

He held on to her small, trembling hand and prayed like he had never prayed before as they went into the living room to catch up with Marsh. The furniture had been turned upside down. Drawers and their contents were strewn over the room. The kitchen and dining room were the same. Broken china and silverware flung across every surface. Chairs were overturned.

They passed the first of two bedrooms, which was Lena's office. Like the other rooms, it had been ransacked, furniture overturned. Files and papers were scattered across the hardwood as if a hurricane had blown through the space.

In the final bedroom—Lena's room—the dresser drawers were tossed in every direction. Framed photographs of the sisters that once sat on the dresser had been crushed on the floor. Lingerie was tossed from one side of the room to the other. The bed covers were torn from the mattress.

Bare feet were visible beyond the end of the bed.

Eva yanked free of his hold and ran to where the victim lay on the floor. She dropped to her knees. His entire body vibrating with fear and tension, Todd crossed the room and crouched beside her. The woman had long brown hair…like Lena. The height and weight were right, as Marsh had said. She wore yoga pants and a bra-like top. Her face was beaten beyond recognition.

Damn these bastards.

For ten full seconds Eva stared at the woman, tears flooding down her cheeks. Todd held his breath and prayed some more.

"It's not her."

Relief rushed through his veins even as regret that someone else's sister or daughter or wife had been murdered tugged at his gut. "You're sure?"

"Look closely," Marsh urged.

"Her hair is too long. Her fingers are thicker than Lena's and her fingernails are too short." Eva drew in a shaky breath. "Lena gets her nails done every week." She gestured to the woman's bare midriff. "Lena has a birthmark on her right side. It looks like a little white cloud." She looked up at Marsh, a shaky smile on her lips even as the tears continued to flow. "She always hated it."

"Okay." Marsh nodded. "Does your sister have a friend or a neighbor with long brown hair?" He looked to the victim. "One who fits what you see here." He shook his head then and looked away.

Eva moved her head side to side. "Lena has so many friends. I'm sorry. I don't know."

Todd helped her to her feet and asked the detective, "We done here?" She'd been through enough. Whatever else Marsh wanted to know he would need to ask Lena.

He nodded. "For now." To Eva he said, "I really am sorry we had to put you through this, Ms. Bowman, but we didn't have a lot of choice. Every minute we waste with red tape is a minute we can't get back. Waiting for the medical examiner to come and remove the body before we let you have a look down at the morgue would have eaten up hours."

Eva took a deep breath. "I understand. I'll let my sister know what's happened."

Marsh had one of his officers bring the Camaro right up in front of the townhouse.

Todd ushered Eva into the car as quickly as possible.

Somewhere amid the crowd, Robles's men would be watching.

Chapter Thirteen

Eva paced the living room. Ian Michaels had delivered her new phone. She had finally reached Lena's boss who called a point of contact in DC that confirmed Lena had an early morning interview. According to the contact in DC, she should be finishing up soon and be available to return Eva's call. Lena's boss assured Eva that it was common for a reporter to shut off his or her cell phone during an important interview. She understood that part—Lena had told her as much on numerous occasions—but the knowledge did nothing to alleviate Eva's mounting concern. She couldn't possibly relax until she heard her sister's voice.

Another woman was dead. Eva couldn't pretend that the woman's life or Mrs. Cackowski's mattered less than her own. She possessed the ability to stop the bloodshed, and putting off that necessary step was unequivocally wrong.

She summoned her courage, folded her arms across her chest and said as much. "I want to meet the person the Colby Agency found who might be willing to speak out against Miguel Robles." She met Todd's startled gaze with lead in her own. "He might be able to help us end this now."

"First," he countered, "leaving this house is growing increasingly dangerous. It's my job to protect you and I take that job very seriously."

When she would have argued, he held up a hand and continued, "Second, allowing you to even know the name of the man who's talking to the agency much less speak with him could shut him down. Even if for some strange reason he agreed to meet with you, some small thing you say or do might change his mind. We can't risk rocking that particular boat right now. He's far too potentially valuable to the investigation."

"You promised we'd talk about what I *can* do." She checked her new cell phone, willing it to ring and growing all the more frustrated when it didn't. "I can't stay hidden forever. I thought you understood my feelings on the matter. So let's stop going over what I can't do and discuss something I can."

Maybe it was wrong to lay a guilt trip on him but she was desperate. If she didn't hear from Lena soon she might just lose it. It was either that or fall apart and she'd done that once already today. Going there again wasn't an option. She needed to be strong and focused. Two people were dead and another was in the hospital because of her. Eva had to do something besides hide and wait.

He opened his mouth to answer and her cell rang. The number for the television station where Lena worked flashed on the screen. A new stab of worry sliced deep into Eva's heart as she accepted the call. "Hello."

"Eva, this is Scott Mason from Channel 7."

Lena's boss. Eva's fingers tightened on the phone. "Did you hear from Lena?"

"Not exactly." He hesitated and Eva's heart fractured. "I spoke to the cameraman who was supposed to be at the interview with her this morning. He said Lena cancelled the interview because she got word that her sister had been in an accident. She left DC around eight this morning. No one has heard from her since."

Eva's world tilted and the crack in her heart widened. "Thank you, Mr. Mason." He was still speaking when Eva ended the call. She couldn't listen to more of his regrets and offers of comfort. She turned to Todd. "Lena came back to Chicago." Outrage roared through her. "I have to find her. Now."

"Give me five minutes. Let me make some calls."

Rather than debate him, Eva sank into the nearest chair. She wanted to believe that this was some sort of misunderstanding. Maybe a friend who'd heard about the explosion at the church had gotten her wires crossed. Maybe the cameraman misunderstood what Lena said when she cancelled the interview. Even as she turned over all the possibilities, every instinct warned that it wasn't a mistake. Lena had been lured back here by that monster Miguel Robles and now she was in trouble. A new surge of fear and pain extinguished the outrage. Her sister could die... she could be dead already.

Todd ended his call and slid the phone back into his pocket. "I've got the agency verifying that Lena boarded a plane headed for Chicago. It'll take a bit of time, but we'll know one way or the other soon enough. Until then, let's keep in mind that Lena is a very savvy investigative journalist. She wouldn't be fooled easily."

Eva dredged up her fleeing courage. She agreed with his statement; it was a valid point, to a degree. "If that's true, then why hasn't she answered my calls or called me back?"

"Her cell battery may need to be charged. She might be on her way to the agency offices as we speak." He crouched in front of her and searched her eyes a moment, his so certain of his words. "Lena is a fighter. If Robles lured her into a trap, he's in for a hell of a surprise."

Eva managed a faint smile. She would love nothing better than to cling to that scenario, but deep in her heart she knew there was only one explanation for why they hadn't heard from Lena. Every ounce of warmth leeched out of her body. "She hasn't called me because she can't call me. And you're right, she is a fighter, but there are some battles even the strongest person can't win. I'm not going to pretend the situation isn't exactly what it is."

He dropped his head for a moment before meeting her eyes once more. "Until we know for certain she's with Robles, we should stay calm and hope for the best."

Eva wanted to laugh at the suggestion but she couldn't form the sound.

Her cell rang.

Eva stared at the device clenched in her right hand. Lena's face and name flashed on the screen. Her heart thumped hard against her ribs. "Lena."

"Eva."

Lena's voice sounded raw and edged with uncertainty. Eva went numb. "Where are you?"

"They want me to tell you where I am so you can come to me."

The undeniable nuance of fear in her sister's voice stole Eva's breath.

"Put it on Speaker," Todd whispered.

Her hand trembling, Eva touched the speaker image on the screen with one icy finger and said, "I can come right now. Just tell me where."

"He told me to tell you that you can't tell anyone, Eva, and no matter what else happens," she said, her words stilted as if she were taking great care with each one, "don't come!" Lena shouted the final two words.

More shouting and scuffling echoed from the speaker. Eva's heart flailed in her chest. "Lena!"

Todd reached for the phone but Eva twisted away from him. "Lena!"

"Your sister is not a very smart woman," a male voice said.

Eva instantly recognized the voice. *Miguel Robles*. Had to be. This was the same voice that had taunted her about the Chavez woman's shooting. "Tell me where she is. I'll come right now."

"I will send you instructions at six thirty this evening," Robles said. "Keep your phone close. If you deviate from my precise instructions, your sister will die."

"I can come now!"

The connection severed.

Eva pushed to her feet, brushed past Todd and stood in the center of the room. She had to think. She turned all the way around. Where was her charger? She needed to make sure her phone battery stayed fully charged. The bastard told her to keep her phone close.

Todd was on his cell, his voice low and quiet. Eva ignored him. It didn't matter to whom he was speaking or what he thought she should do; she was doing exactly what Robles told her to do. She would not risk Lena's life under any circumstance. Whatever Robles asked her to do, she would do it. Defeat and certainty settled deep into her bones.

This moment had been coming all week. Fighting it any longer was futile.

"Michaels has a friend at NSA."

Eva dragged her thoughts from the haze

of worry and struggled to focus on the man staring at her with such immense concern. "How will that help us?" A numbness had taken over. She felt as though she were under water. She could see and hear but it was all distorted and so far away. The moment felt surreal…as if it were happening to someone else and Eva was only watching.

"NSA can track any cell phone. They can determine in minutes what it takes others days to figure out. That call from Lena's phone will give us what we need. We find the phone and we'll find her. The way I see it, we have a little better than five hours to find her before Robles makes a move."

"I will not take any chances with my sister's life." Eva lifted her chin in defiance of whatever he might have in mind. "I hired you. I can fire you. Unless we do this my way."

"I agree completely." He reached for Eva's free hand. "But for the next five hours I need you to trust me. I've carried out a lot of high-risk rescues. I know what I'm doing."

Eva searched for calm. He had been in Special Forces and the Colby Agency was the best in the business of private investigations and security. "What's your plan?"

He visibly relaxed. "First we find the location the call was made from. Robles was careful. He kept the call short. He feels confident we won't be able to trace him. And he's right, we can't. But there are people who can."

Eva had heard about the NSA's ability to track the cell phones of suspected terrorists but that was the extent of her knowledge on the subject. "How can we be certain the location is accurate?"

"Lena uses a smartphone. At this very minute her phone is attempting to locate cell towers and Wi-Fi hot spots. NSA can narrow her location down to a city block or less within the hour. We will find her and then we'll get her out—safe."

For a moment Eva wanted to argue with him. This was her sister—the only family she had in this world. Eva would do anything to make sure she stayed safe just as Lena would do anything for her. She'd told Eva not to come. Her sister would without hesitation willingly die for her.

But this wasn't about Lena. This was about Eva and if anyone else was going to die today, it would be her.

West 47th Street, 5:40 p.m.

ROBLES CHOSE THE home field advantage. The Back of the Yards neighborhood was one of

Chicago's most notorious where more residents than not felt the city had abandoned them, leaving gangs to take over. Century-old houses and aging apartment buildings butted up to derelict warehouses and industrial buildings that once infused life into the economy that was now dying. The handful of determined business owners hanging on to their small shops and slivers of new development and refurbishment continued to provide a glimmer of hope for change, but little actually changed.

Robles wasn't the only one at home along the most dangerous streets of the Windy City. Todd had done some time here. From age fifteen to sixteen he'd lived with a foster family on the fringes of this neglected, gang-infested territory. The mom-and-pop shops had been his favorite haunts, the rail tracks and the boxcars his playground.

The commercial equipment rental company that Robles and his men had taken over for the evening's event extended a full city block. Compressors, backhoes and excavators lined the parking lot behind the security fence. Warehouses and the main office formed a boundary on three sides, leaving only the front with its ten-foot-high fence to afford a visual onto the property. Directly across the street was the rail yard, and behind the rental compound was a street lined with trees and more of those early twentieth-century bungalows built by immigrants and stockyard workers.

Way too many people lived around the target to go in without backup from Chicago PD. Eva hadn't taken the news well. He'd had a hell of a time talking her out of walking away from his protection. Her concerns about involving the police were understandable but hardly reasonable. Ultimately, they'd reached a standoff and he'd called Marsh. Eva had told Todd in no uncertain terms how she felt about his decision.

If this operation went to hell and her sister was hurt or worse, it was on him.

"We have eyes all around the property," Sergeant Carter assured them now. "We've quietly evacuated residents for two blocks in either direction."

"We're making sure none of the evacuees uses a cell phone until this is over in an effort to ensure no one alerts Robles's people," Marsh added. "We're keeping the folks entertained over at St. Joseph's on Hermitage."

Eva shook her head, her doubts about how this would go down clear. "If any of his men spot a cop—"

"Don't worry, Ms. Bowman," Carter said, "we've got this. We've even got unmarked units monitoring traffic all around our position."

To Todd's surprise Eva didn't say another word. Instead, she walked around the corner of the double boxcar and stared through the bushes and trees separating the rail yard from the street. If her sister was with her cell phone as they believed, she was likely no more than twenty, twenty-five yards in front of where Eva stood. Todd tried to think of something reassuring to say as he followed that same path.

"He's going to call or text me with instructions and they'll go in." She shook her head and hugged her arms more tightly around herself. "This plan is too risky. I'm not willing to risk Lena's life this way."

"Do you really believe Robles will let Lena go if you surrender yourself?" They'd been over this same territory twice already and her answer was always the same.

"It's a risk I have to take."

Todd glanced back toward the huddle of cops. He hadn't planned to share the other op already in motion with her until they had eyes on Lena. At this point he would do just about anything to give Eva some sense of relief.

"Marsh and the others don't know that we have a two-man team working their way inside." Her shoulders stiffened as he spoke, but she kept her attention straight ahead. "They were already here," he went on, "and in place before Chicago PD developed their game plan and moved in."

For the first time since he told Eva the Colby Agency had coordinated with Chicago PD after Robles's call, she looked him in the eye. A faint glimmer of hope stirred in hers. "Can they see what's happening inside?"

"They have eyes in the main office. So far they haven't seen Lena but they've watched two men going in and out of an inner office. We believe Lena and Robles are in that office. His disciples are scattered all over the property. All heavily armed."

"I don't understand why he would put himself in this position." Her gaze shifted back across the street. "He must have known there was a chance I would go to the police. How does he expect to escape when all hell breaks loose?" She shook her head. "It feels like a setup. Her phone might very well be here, but Robles and Lena could be anywhere."

Todd glanced at Marsh and Carter who had separated from the main huddle and appeared to be in deep conversation. "We're prepared for that move as well. Michaels is standing by to take us wherever we need to go."

His phone vibrated. Todd pulled it from his hip pocket. The name *Jim Colby*, Victoria's son and head of field operations at the agency, appeared on the screen. Todd's gut clenched as he answered the phone. This couldn't be good news. "What's happening inside?"

"Robles's troops are leaving."

As if on cue the large gate across the street slid open and a line of pimped-out automobiles rolled onto the street. Dread congealed in Todd's gut. "All of them?"

"Every damned one our scouts can see from their vantage points have picked up their weapons and walked out."

"What about the ones you can't see?" Todd resisted the urge to race across the street and yank one of the bastards out of a car and beat the truth out of him. The whole damned parade moved nice and slow as if they wanted those watching to get a good look at the show.

"We're working on getting eyes into that room from a ceiling vent."

"Hello."

Todd turned at the sound of Eva's voice. Her eyes were wide with fear as she listened to the caller. Todd checked the time. Robles was early by fifteen minutes.

"Hold on," he said to Jim.

Eva drew the phone from her ear and stared at the screen, her hand shaking.

"What did he say?"

"He said further instructions are coming by text and that he's sending me a photo of Lena."

The call to Eva's cell had drawn Marsh and Carter. They both looked to Todd. "I'm putting you on speaker, Jim." He set his phone to Speaker and moved closer to Eva to watch for the message from Robles.

The text appeared on her screen.

Your sister is waiting across the street from where you are standing. You have five minutes before she dies.

A photo appeared on the screen.

Lena was gagged, blindfolded and tied to an office chair with a package strapped around her chest. On the package was a clock counting down the seconds.

Bomb.

Chapter Fourteen

"We need the bomb squad! Now! Do not let her move!"

Eva heard Todd's words but her brain refused to assimilate the meaning behind them. She stared at the photo of Lena. Tears had dragged streaks of mascara past the blindfold and down her cheeks to melt into the gag tied around her mouth.

Bomb.

A bomb was strapped to her sister's body.

Todd, Sergeant Carter and several police officers rushed across the street. Detective Marsh gripped Eva by the arm. "Let's move back behind the rail cars."

Eva stared at him for two or three seconds and then she looked back across the street to the men now disappearing into the center building of the equipment rental company.

Lena was in there.

Bomb.

Eva jerked out of the detective's grip and ran. She sprinted across the street.

A horn blared. She lunged forward and the car whipped left, barely avoiding hitting her. Adrenaline fired through her veins. Her heart soared into her throat but she didn't slow. She had to get to her sister.

She reached the building the others had gone into before Marsh caught up with her. She wrenched open the door and rushed inside with him shouting for her to stop.

Can't stop. Gotta get to Lena!

Cops stood seemingly frozen all around the room on this side of a long service counter. Behind the counter, a door stood open. All eyes were on that door.

Sergeant Carter suddenly appeared in the doorway. "Everyone out of the building! Now!"

While the others hurried to obey the sergeant's order, Eva sprinted for the counter. She dodged Marsh as he reached for her again. She rounded the end of the counter and reached the door to find Carter blocking her path to the office and to Lena.

"You need to go with the others," he ordered.

"Get out of my way," she demanded, fear

and anger making her shake so hard her teeth nearly chattered.

For one long moment the man stared at her. Whether he sympathized with her plight or simply didn't want to waste time arguing, he stepped aside.

Eva moved around him and into the office. Her heart sank to her feet as she watched a man clad completely in black and whom she didn't recognize remove the gag from her sister's mouth. The blindfold was already gone.

Lena's fear-filled gaze collided with hers. "Get out of here, Eva!" she cried.

Eva moved forward but the man attending to Lena stopped her with an upraised hand. "Don't touch her. We don't know what might trigger the detonator."

Todd was on the phone explaining what the bomb looked like, she assumed to someone from the bomb squad.

She swallowed hard. Help couldn't possibly make it in time.

Eva eased as close as she dared to her sister. "I'm so sorry." Hot tears spilled down her cheeks as she watched the readout on the clock go from 2:00 to 1:59.

Please don't let his happen.

Another man dressed in black burst into the room. "Wire snips!" He handed the tool to Todd. She realized then that the two men in black were probably the two from the Colby Agency who had infiltrated the building.

Lena smiled up at Eva, her lips trembling with the effort. "I love you, little sister, and I appreciate that you're sorry but you need to go. If we both die, he wins."

Eva dropped to her knees next to Lena and dared to take her hand. "Then let him win."

Todd glanced at her for one second before reaching into the mass of colored wires and snipping one.

1:29

He moved to another as the voice on the phone instructed, she presumed. "Please leave, Eva," he murmured as he reached for the tangle of wires again.

"Sorry." She drew in a shaky breath. "Can't do it." Nothing could make her leave the two people she loved most in the world.

Todd swore and snipped the second wire.

1:18...1:17

"This is not working," he muttered.

Eva thought of all the wonderful times she and her sister had shared. Of how much she loved and missed their parents...and she thought of Todd and how she had missed him...how she loved him so much her heart wanted to burst even now—particularly now.

He was prepared to give his life for Lena. He was a hero. He'd always been one, she'd just been too hurt to see it.

In that terrifying moment one truth crystalized for Eva. She should have gone after him. All this time she had been angry and crushed because he'd left and not once had she considered going after him. She had been well aware of how difficult his childhood was. She should have recognized that he might have trouble committing and tracked him down and demanded answers. Pride had kept her from taking that step.

"If my cameraman was here," Lena said as more tears slipped down her blackened cheeks, "this would make a hell of a breaking news story." Lena laughed but the sound held no humor.

Eva nodded. "You can tell Channel 7 viewers the whole story on the late news tonight."

Lena gifted her with another of those shaky smiles. "Absolutely."

Carter rushed back into the room with a larger tool. Using what appeared to be large pruning shears or maybe bolt cutters, he and the man standing next to Lena attempted to cut through the thick nylon straps holding her and the bomb bound to the chair.

0:59

Fear tightened its ruthless grip on Eva.
Hurry!

Lena squeezed her hand and whispered,
"Please go."

Eva shook her head and held her sister's
hand even tighter. "No way."

"Hold on a minute," Todd said to the man
on the phone. "Something isn't right."

The bottom dropped out of Eva's stomach.
Oh no. What now?

0:42

Carter and the other man Eva believed
to be from the Colby Agency carefully cut
through another of the straps as Todd explained something about the bomb that Eva
couldn't hope to comprehend.

Her heart fluttered so wildly she felt light-
headed as the men cut away a third strap.
Please, please hurry.

Todd suddenly tossed his phone aside. It
slid across the tile floor as he grabbed the re-
mainder of the wires and yanked them free
of the box.

0:19

Eva held her breath.

Lena's face paled to a ghostly white.

Todd gripped the box and pulled. The face
of the box as well as the clock came loose in
his hands.

Inside the black box strapped to Lena's chest there was nothing.

It was empty.

"Son of a bitch," Todd muttered.

The last strap fell away from Lena. Eva scrambled to her feet as the man in black whose name she didn't know helped Lena out of the chair. Lena's knees gave way and he scooped her into his arms.

"Get everyone out!" Todd commanded.

Before Eva could ask what was happening now, the double doors of a large cabinet on the other side of the room burst open. What the hell?

Eva saw the weapon first, then the man. The scream that filled the air was hers; she couldn't seem to stop the sound.

He leveled the barrel of the weapon on her. "Die, bitch!"

The blast exploded, shaking the air in the room.

Todd's body slammed into her where she stood frozen to the spot.

They crashed onto the floor. Eva grunted as the breath burst from her lungs.

Lena's mouth opened in a scream.

Time lapsed into slow motion...drawing out the sound of her sister's scream. Other voices shouted but Eva couldn't make out the seemingly distorted words.

The man with the gun charged forward, his face contorted with hatred, his weapon still in his hand.

The eerie quiet was ruptured by one, two, three more gunshots.

Then there was silence again.

Eva dragged in a breath, the sound shattering the dreamlike slow motion.

Todd moved off her. "You okay?"

His voice sounded strangely far away.

Eva tried to nod but her head bobbled. She felt disconnected and tattered.

The muffled sound of Lena crying came from somewhere.

There was blood…so much blood.

"He's down," Sergeant Carter said.

"We need an ambulance," someone else said, one of the men wearing black maybe.

Eva looked first at Lena. No blood. She was okay. The man who'd been holding her had stood her on her feet and was now providing directions for the ambulance.

Eva stared at her bloody T-shirt. Where was all the blood coming from? Had she been shot? She was reasonably sure not, but considering the sluggish way her senses were reacting she wasn't certain of anything.

The man who'd come out of that cabinet intending to shoot her lay on the floor a few feet away, his eyes open, a bullet hole in the center of his forehead.

Todd reached down to her.

She stared at the wide hand and fingers that had touched her body and soul. The blood smeared on his palm showed her what she hadn't wanted to see.

She hadn't been shot…it was Todd. Blood had soaked into his shirt. The bullet appeared to have hit his left upper arm in the area of the deltoid muscle.

Hers shaking, she took his hand and got to her feet. "Oh my God. You're…"

He grinned. "It's nothing. Besides, I know an excellent nurse."

The Edge, 9:00 p.m.

TODD FLINCHED.

Dr. Marissa Frasier smiled. "Good thing that was the last one." She finished the final suture and stepped back from the exam table.

"Thanks, Doc." Todd moved his arm, wincing at the pain.

Frasier peeled off her gloves and tossed them into the trash receptacle. "The nurse will be in shortly and she'll bandage that for you. Thank you, Mr. Christian, for keeping Eva safe. She means a great deal to all of us."

Todd gave the lady a nod. When she'd left the room he exhaled a big breath. He'd never felt more tired in his life. He closed his eyes. Those few minutes with that clock ticking down had been the longest and most terrifying of his life. If Eva or Lena had...

No. He couldn't think about that. It was over. They were both fine. He was fine. The nightmare was over.

The door opened and he looked up, his heart lifting in expectation.

"Looks like you're good to go," Lena said.

"No worse for the wear," he returned, tension rifling through him. He'd expected Eva to walk through that door or maybe one of the other nurses. Lena was about the last person he'd figured he would see again tonight. Didn't she have a hot breaking story to report?

She folded her arms over her chest and stared at him for a long moment. He braced for all hell to break loose.

"You broke my sister's heart when you left."

He couldn't deny the charge. "I won't offer you an excuse because I don't have one. I was a coward who didn't deserve her."

She looked surprised at his confession "A coward for sure. And a jerk as well as a—"

He held up a hand. "I was all those things, yes. I've apologized to Eva."

Lena threw her head back and laughed. When she finally regained her composure, she said, "I love my sister more than anything else in this world. You hurt her again and I will make you wish you had never come back to Chicago."

He nodded. "Got it."

She turned and stepped toward the door. Her hand on the handle, she hesitated a second or two before turning back to him. "Thank you." She stared at the floor before meeting his gaze once more. "It's a rare man who would willingly give his life while trying to save another. Whatever you were ten years ago, you're a good man now. I saw that today."

A smile spread across his lips. "Thank you. Hearing you say that means a lot."

She pointed a finger at him. "But I'll still kick your ass if you hurt her."

With that she left the room. Kim came in next and bandaged his freshly sutured wound while going over the care instructions the doctor had left.

"There you go, Mr. Christian." She handed

him his discharge papers. "You're all done." She sighed. "It's a little crazy tonight so we had to put Eva to work. She told me to tell you that if you didn't want to wait she would understand."

Todd hopped off the table. "I'll wait."

Kim flashed him a grin and said, "I thought you might." With that, she hurried out the door to move on to the next patient.

He'd waited a long time to have Eva back in his life. What was a few more hours?

West Grace Street Apartments, Midnight

EVA CHECKED HER door one last time. Locked. She pressed her forehead to the cool surface and thought of Mrs. Cackowski's door across the hall. However longer Eva lived in this building, on this floor, she would never be able to pass that door without thinking of the sweet lady. Eva hoped Miguel Robles died screaming for what he'd done. With Lena's help the police had identified the murdered woman found in her town house. She had worked at a coffee shop down the street from where Lena lived. Robles's people had likely chosen her because she and Lena had similar features. *Bastards.*

Another innocent victim slain for no other reason except to terrify Eva.

But Miguel Robles wasn't getting away with his heinous deeds anymore. The police had found him with the help of their new informant, thanks to the Colby Agency. Robles had been so certain that his chosen assassin would kill both Eva and Lena, he had personally and boldly tortured Lena with promises that both she and Eva would die today—all as he held her hostage. With the informant's testimony as well as Lena's, Robles was done. He would spend the rest of his life in prison.

"I'm starving."

Eva turned away from the door and smiled at her hero. "If you'll give me a moment to change, I'll prepare you the most amazing meal you've ever eaten."

It was the least she could do after he'd saved her life. Her heart squeezed. He'd taken the bullet meant for her. He'd kept her safe and protected her through this entire nightmare. Now he had matching bandages, one on his right shoulder, the other on his left upper arm. Poor guy.

At his skeptical look, she said, "I've become quite the chef since college."

Propped against her kitchen counter, his

gorgeous chest bare, he grinned. "Been keeping secrets, have you?"

He'd tossed his shirt at the hospital. She'd been so damn glad the bullet hadn't caused any real damage she wouldn't have cared if he'd walked out of there naked. Every female in the vicinity had swooned as he walked by as it was. She'd had to help out with the Saturday night rush for a couple of hours and Todd had stationed himself where he could watch. Every time she glanced at him she saw the hunger in his eyes, but she was pretty sure it had nothing to do with food. Her entire being tingled with anticipation.

"I have," she confessed. "A woman should always have at least a few secrets." She headed for the bathroom. "Relax. I'll only be a minute."

Shutting herself away in the room that now felt like a closet compared to the bathroom she'd had at the Colby safe house, she stared at herself in the mirror for a long moment. "What're you doing, Eva?"

She'd insisted on bringing Todd home with her. He shouldn't be alone. He had been shot after all. But that had been an excuse. This wasn't about taking care of him for the night or even showing her gratitude for his protection. This was far more.

She wasn't ready to let him go. When Kim had told her that he intended to wait while Eva helped out, her heart had started to beat so fast she could hardly stay focused on her work. He was here and there were things she needed to say. Before Lena left the hospital tonight she had made Eva promise that she would tell Todd the truth. Apparently her big sister had recognized that truth just watching the two of them together.

You're still in love with him.

Eva had denied Lena's accusation. She'd spent the better part of the past decade pretending she hated him. She peeled off her scrub top and shimmied out of the bottom and tossed both aside. She'd changed out of her bloody clothes at the hospital to help out. Sometimes sudden bursts of incoming patients happened like that, especially on the weekends.

Eva drew in a reaffirming breath. Lena was right. Eva did love Todd. She hoped her sister was right about the other as well. Lena was convinced that Todd still loved Eva. Eva wasn't so sure. Yes, Todd had stepped in front of a bullet for her, but that had been his job.

She thought of the way he touched her. The way he had apologized for leaving, admitting that he'd been afraid he didn't deserve her.

Maybe he did still care for her. Her mother had sworn he would be back.

"Stop." Eva shook her head. She was setting herself up for major heartbreak. Time to give it a rest. She would know soon enough how he felt. Frankly she was surprised Lena hadn't scared him off with her warning. If Eva hadn't been so busy with patients, she would have headed off that awkward scene.

He'd taken Lena's scolding and still waited for Eva. That was something. She ran a brush through her hair before going to her closet where she shuffled through the offerings until she found another tee and a pair of lounge pants. What she really needed was a shower, but Todd was hungry and she didn't want to make him wait.

A knock at her door was followed by, "Hey, I found what I really wanted."

"Oh yeah?" she asked as he opened the door. Holding the tee and pants to her body as if she needed to hide the fact that she was standing there in panties and a bra, she beamed a smile she hoped covered for the worrisome thoughts nagging at her. "Can't wait for a decent meal, eh?"

He held up the chocolate frosting as he took a step toward her. "I decided I wanted to go straight to dessert."

Her skin felt on fire. "You're an injured man." She tossed the clothes aside. This was one aspect of their relationship where she had nothing to hide from him. "I'm not sure you're up for dessert."

He licked his lips and her nipples stung. "I think I can hold my own."

She reached behind her and unfastened her bra, letting it fall forward, revealing her breasts before falling into a wisp of lace on the floor. "There are things we need to talk about."

Another step disappeared between them. Her breath caught. No other man had ever made her wet by just walking toward her. How could she possibly ever deny how much she loved this man? She loved every perfectly sculpted inch of him. His gorgeous body, scars and all. That handsome face. Blue, blue eyes and lips so kissable her mouth ached to taste them. That thick hair she loved running her fingers through.

"What kind of things?" he asked.

And that voice. So deep, it wrapped around her and made her want to close her eyes and fall into the sound.

He stood right in front of her now, waiting for her answer to his question. "Like," she stammered, "what *this* is?"

The way he looked at her—as if he intended to devour her rather than the chocolate—she knew she was in trouble.

"This," he murmured in that steamy, sexy voice as he moved closer and closer, forcing her to step back until he'd backed her all the way to the bed, "is me wanting you so badly I can barely breathe."

He moved in another step and she dropped onto the bed, scooted out of his reach. He tossed the chocolate onto the covers and climbed onto the bed on all fours, crawling slowly toward her.

"This is us taking back what I let slip away before." He moved over her, lowered his mouth to hers and kissed her so softly she whimpered with the sweetness of it. "I ran away before because I was afraid." His lips hovered just centimeters above hers. "I swear to you I'm not afraid anymore. I'm here to stay, if you'll have me."

She reached up and nipped at his lips. "I might need a little more convincing."

He grinned, his lips brushing hers. "Happy to oblige."

He sat back on his heels and reached for the frosting. He tore open the package and dipped his finger into the luscious chocolate. Slowly, he traced a path down her throat and around her breasts, tipping each nipple with the sweet stuff before dipping down to her belly button. He leaned down and traced that path with his tongue. It was all she could do to bear the exquisite torture. She shivered and moaned, reminding herself to breathe as her fingers fisted in the covers.

He moved slowly, savoring the chocolate as he went. Then he made a new path, this one right down to the waistband of her lacy panties. He dragged the strappy lace down her legs and off before crawling back up her body until he reached her belly button. As he teased her belly button with his mouth, he stroked her inner thighs with his fingers, tortured her clitoris, pushing her beyond her limits.

By the time he reached for his fly she was writhing with need. "Hurry," she whispered.

She helped him push his jeans down his lean hips and then guide himself into her. With her legs locked around his, she closed her eyes and melted with the feel of him filling her body so completely.

He kissed her cheek, tracing a path to her ear as he held his body too damn still. "I love you, Eva," he whispered.

She stared into his eyes, trailing her fingers

down his sinewy torso and wrapped her arms around his waist. "I love you, Todd."

The rest of what they had to say, they said with their bodies.

Chapter Fifteen

Sunday, May 13, 9:00 a.m.

Victoria sipped her hot tea and smiled. Her husband was doing what he always did on Sunday morning: reading the newspaper while his second cup of coffee cooled. She and Lucas Camp had been friends for most of their lives, husband and wife for a good number of years now.

When she studied him like this, she wondered how it was possible to love him more each day, but she did. Ten or so years ago they had decided to retire. They'd even moved to the warmer climate of Texas and pretended to relax for a while. But that hadn't worked out so well. The Colby Agency was too much a part of the fabric of their lives. Cold, windy Chicago was as well. Their children and grandchildren were here. The worst tragedies of their lives as well as the happiest days of their lives had all played out right here. After only a few months away they had made a mutual decision to return and to never again leave their beloved home.

The two of them would go into the office Monday through Friday until they drew their last breaths. Lucas still consulted on cases with his old team at the CIA. He and Thomas Casey, the former director of Lucas's shadow unit, still had lunch once a month. It was hard to let go of a life's work, and the powers that be still needed old-school spies like Lucas and Thomas.

Victoria felt immensely grateful that she and Lucas spent most of their time helping others. Life could be so difficult sometimes. They were both committed to seeing that her son Jim and Lucas's son Slade followed in their footsteps. The Colby Agency had become a cornerstone of Chicago; that legacy must be carried on.

Victoria smiled. "I'm very pleased with Jamie's ability to work without supervision. She's learning quickly to anticipate the necessary steps in a case."

Lucas folded the newspaper and set it aside. "It's refreshing to see such ambition in a young lady her age."

Victoria set her teacup aside. "I hope Luke

is as excited about following in his father's and his grandparents' shoes as his older sister."

Lucas laughed. "Give the boy time. Girls mature much faster than boys."

Victoria had to laugh. "This is very true."

The sparkle of mischief in her husband's gray eyes made her smile. "But our women love us anyway."

"We do, indeed." She could not imagine her life without this man. They were two of a kind. "Tell me, did you discover anything useful in your search into Dr. Pierce's past?"

Dr. Devon Pierce, former renowned surgeon and the genius behind the Edge facility, had a ghost from his past haunting his newly found success. He'd ignored it for some time but when he and Victoria had been discussing Eva Bowman's troubles, Pierce had confessed to having a problem of his own.

Lucas raised his cup to his lips, savoring the bold flavor of his favorite blend. When he'd placed the cup in its saucer once more, he considered her question a moment longer. "Pierce's background is littered with tragedy."

Victoria was aware of his personal tragedy. He and his wife had been visiting her family in Binghamton, New York, for the holidays when an awful car accident left her gravely injured. Pierce had been severely injured himself and the local hospital simply wasn't equipped to handle their needs. With no time to wait for his wife to be airlifted to another hospital and no surgeon available to help her, Pierce had tried to save her himself. She died on the operating table.

Eventually he had returned to work as the head of surgery at Chicago's prestigious Rush University Medical Center. Within a year he had resigned to focus solely on reinventing the Emergency Department. Six years later his creation, the Edge, was the prototype for new facilities all over the country.

As much as Victoria respected Devon Pierce, she felt sympathy for him as well. He had not allowed himself to have a real life since his wife died. Work was his only companion. He continued to live alone in the massive mansion in Lake Bluff he'd built for her. Victoria and Lucas had been to his home once, before he lost his wife. They'd hosted a fund-raiser for a new wing at Rush. The Georgian-style mansion had been more like a castle than a home.

How sad that such a brilliant and caring man refused to open his heart again.

"You didn't find anything that might have

fostered trouble in his career since developing the Edge?"

Lucas propped his elbows on the table and clasped his hands in front of him. "Not yet, but, my dear, you know as well as I do that you don't rise to the top in anything without leaving a few skeletons in your closet."

Her husband was full of sage proverbs this morning. "Then we must find the one doing the rattling."

Lucas gave her a nod. "You have the perfect investigator for the job."

"Isabella Lytle," Victoria agreed.

"Shall we schedule breakfast with Bella in the morning to discuss the case?"

Victoria reached across the table for her cell phone. "I'll send her a text now."

Once Dr. Pierce's troubles were resolved, perhaps he would finally let go of the past and live the life he continued to ignore in the present.

As if he'd sensed her thought, Lucas laid his hand on hers. "Don't worry, my dear, the Colby Agency never fails a client."

That was one truth she intended to spend the rest of her life backing up.

* * * * *

*Read on for an excerpt of
SIN AND BONE, another sexy*
COLBY AGENCY: SEXI-ER *story,
coming next month from Debra Webb
and Harlequin Intrigue!*

SIN AND BONE

Chapter One

Dr. Devon Pierce listened as administrators from more than a dozen hospitals in metropolitan areas across the nation bemoaned the increasing difficulty of maintaining Emergency Departments. Devon was the featured speaker once the opening discussion concluded.

He rarely agreed to speak to committees and groups even in a teleconference such as today's when his appearance required only that he remain in his office and speak to the monitor on his desk. He much preferred to remain focused on his work at the Edge. There were times, however, when his participation in the world of research and development was required in order to push those who still stumbled in the darkness toward the light of the most advanced medical technologies. Emergency treatment centers like the Edge were the future of emergency medicine. There was no other more state-of-the-art facility.

Devon had spent six years developing the concept before opening the prototype in his hometown of Chicago. The success of the past year provided significant evidence of all that he believed about the future of emergency rooms. This would be his legacy to the work he loved.

The subject of cost reared its inevitable and unpleasant head in the ongoing discussion as it always did. How could one measure the worth of saving a human life? He said as much to those listening eagerly for a comment from him. All involved were aware, perhaps to varying degrees, just how much his dedication to his work had cost him. He'd long ago stopped keeping account. His work required what it required. There were no other factors or concerns to weigh.

Half an hour later, Devon had scarcely uttered his closing remarks when the door to his office opened soundlessly. Patricia Ezell, his secretary, moved to his desk. She passed him a note, not the sort of news he wanted to learn if her worried expression was any indicator, and it generally was.

You're needed in the OR stat.

"I'm afraid I won't be able to take any questions. Duty calls." Devon severed his connection to the conference and stood. "What's going on?" he asked as he closed a single button on his suit jacket.

Patricia shook her head. "Dr. Reagan rushed a patient into surgery in OR 1. He says he needs you there."

Ice hardened in Devon's veins. "Reagan is well aware that I don't—"

"He has the surgery under control, Dr. Pierce. It's…" Patricia took a deep breath. "The patient was unconscious when the paramedics brought her in. Her driver's license identifies her as Cara Pierce."

A spear of pain arrowed through Devon, making him hesitate. He closed his laptop. "Few of us have a name so unique that it's not shared with others." There were likely numerous Cara Pierces in the country. Chicago was a large city. Of course, there would be other people with the same name as his late wife. This should be no surprise to the highly trained and, frankly, brilliant members of his staff.

"One of the registration specialists browsed

the contacts list in her cell phone and called the number listed as Husband."

Devon hesitated once more, this time at the door. His secretary's reluctance to provide whatever other details about this patient at her disposal had grown increasingly tedious. "Is her husband en route?"

Patricia cleared her throat. "Based on the number in her contacts list, her husband is already here. The number is *yours*." She held out his cell phone. "I took the call."

Devon stared at the thin, sleek device in her hand. He'd left his cell with Patricia for the duration of the teleconference. His distaste for any distraction, particularly those of cell phones, was an admitted pet peeve of his. He reached for it now. "Thank you, Patricia. Ask the paramedic who brought her in to drop by my office when he has a break."

The walk from his office in the admin wing to the Surgery unit took all of two minutes. One of the finely tuned features of the Edge design was ensuring that each wing of the Emergency Department was never more than two to three minutes away from anything else. A great deal of planning had gone into the round design of the building with the care initiation front and center and the less urgent care units spanning into different wings around the circle. The very center, rear portion of the design contained the more urgent services, imaging and surgery. Every square foot of the facility was designed for optimum efficiency. Each member of the staff was carefully chosen and represented the very best in their field.

As he neared the surgery suite, he considered what his secretary had told him about the patient. The mere idea was absurd. Without a doubt there was a mistake. A mix-up of some sort.

Cara.

Devon banished memories of his wife. Cara was dead. He'd buried her six years and eight months ago.

Two of the three operating rooms were empty. Devon moved into the observation area where all three rooms, spanning in a half circle, could be viewed. He touched the keypad and the black tint of the glass that made up the top half of the wall all the way around the observation area cleared, allowing him to see and those in the OR to see him. The patient's hair was covered with the usual generic cap, preventing him from identifying the color. Most of her face was obscured by the oxygen mask. He turned on the audio in OR 1.

"Evening, Dr. Pierce," Reagan said without glancing up, his hands moving quickly in a perfectly orchestrated rhythm that was all too familiar to Devon.

"Dr. Reagan." Devon's fingers twitched as he watched the finely choreographed dance around the patient.

"Splenic rupture. Concussion but no bleeding that we've found." Reagan remained focused on the video screen as he manipulated the laparoscopic instruments to resect and suture the damaged organ. "She'll be a little bruised and unhappy about the small surgical scars we'll leave behind, but otherwise, she should be as good as new before you know it."

Five or ten seconds elapsed before Devon could respond or move to go. "Watch for intracerebral hemorrhaging." He switched off the audio, darkened the glass once more and walked away.

His wife had died of intracerebral hemorrhaging. There had been no one to save her and his efforts had been too late.

But this woman was not his wife.

Devon drew in a deep breath and returned to his office. Patricia glanced up at him as he passed her desk but he said nothing. With his office door closed he moved to the window overlooking the meticulously manicured grounds. He stared at nothing in particular for a long while. When his mind and pulse rate had calmed sufficiently, he settled behind his desk. A couple of clicks of the keyboard opened the patient portal. He pulled up the patient chart for the woman he'd observed in surgery.

Pierce, Cara Reese, 37. Her address was listed as the Lake Bluff residence Devon had built for his wife...the house he had inhabited *alone* for the past six-plus years.

He scrolled down the file to a copy of her driver's license.

His breath trapped in his lungs.

Blond hair, blue eyes. Height, five-six. Weight, one ten. Date of birth, November tenth—all the statistics matched the ones that would have been found on Cara's license. But it was the photo that proved the most shocking of all. Silky hair brushed her shoulders. Mischief sparkled in her eyes.

The woman in the photo was Cara. *His Cara.*

Devon was on his feet before his brain assimilated to the fact that he had stood. The DMV photo was the same one from the last time his wife renewed her license eight years ago. As if that September morning happened only yesterday, he recalled vividly when she realized her driver's license had expired. She'd been so busy with her new project at the Children's Center, she'd completely forgotten. He'd teased her relentlessly.

His chest screamed for oxygen, forcing him to draw in a tight breath. The name could certainly be chalked up to pure coincidence. The photo...that was an entirely different story.

A rap on his door pulled him back to the present. Devon reluctantly shifted his attention there. Why wasn't Patricia handling visitors? He needed time to untangle this odd mystery. At the sound of another knock he called, "Come in."

The door opened and a young man stuck his head inside. "You wanted to see me, Dr. Pierce?"

Devon didn't recognize the face but the uniform was as familiar as his own reflection, maybe more so since he hadn't scrutinized himself in a mirror in years. More than six, to be exact. The contrasting navy trousers and light blue shirt marked his visitor as a member of the Elite Ambulance service. The identifying badge above the breast pocket confirmed Devon's assessment.

"You brought in the female patient from the automobile accident?"

He nodded. "My partner and I. Yes, sir.

It appeared to be a one-car accident on the Kennedy Expressway near Division. It was the strangest thing."

Devon gestured to the pair of chairs in front of his desk and the young man took a seat. The badge clipped onto his pocket sported the name Warren Eckert. "Strange in what way, Mr. Eckert?"

Devon lowered into his own chair as Eckert spoke. "Nobody witnessed the accident. There was a sizeable dent on the front driver's-side fender, but nothing to suggest the kind of injuries the patient sustained."

"What kind of vehicle was she driving?"

"A brand-new Lexus. Black. Fully loaded." Eckert whistled, long and low. "Sharp car for sure."

Just like Cara's car.

"Do you recall seeing anything in the vehicle besides your patient? Luggage perhaps, or a briefcase?"

Eckert shook his head. "I don't recall. Sorry."

"What about the officers investigating the scene?" Obviously the police had been there, probably before Eckert arrived.

"Joe Telly was the only cop on the scene. He called us before he called backup."

"The woman was not conscious when you arrived?"

"No, sir."

"Was she able to speak to the officer before your arrival?" Devon's instincts were humming. How had a woman involved in such a seemingly minor accident been injured so severely?

"She was unconscious when Telly pulled over to check on her."

"How would you describe the woman?" Devon thought about the photo on the driver's license. "I'm sure you concluded an approximate age and such."

The other man nodded. "Blond hair, blue eyes. Medium height. Kind of thin. Midthirties, I'd say."

"Well dressed?" Her clothes had been removed before surgery and very little of her body had been visible on the operating table.

Eckert nodded slowly. "She was wearing a dress. A short black one. Like she might have been headed to a party or dinner out or something. Not the kind of outfit you'd wear to work unless you're a hostess in an upscale restaurant or something like that."

"Thank you, Mr. Eckert." Devon stood. "I appreciate your time."

"Do you know her?"

The rumor had already made the rounds. "No. I don't."

When the paramedic had exited the office, Devon pulled up the record on this Cara Pierce…this woman who could not be his wife.

Preliminary tox screen showed no drugs. And yet if there was no intracerebral hemorrhaging, why had she still been unconscious when she arrived at the ER? Remaining unconscious for an extended period generally indicated a serious injury, illness or drug use.

Devon picked up his cell phone and made the call he should have made weeks ago. When she answered he dove straight into what needed to be said without preamble. "Victoria, I was mistaken. I will require your services after all."

His old friend Victoria Colby-Camp agreed to have her investigator meet him at his residence at eight tonight.

Devon ended the call and tossed his phone onto his desk. Last month someone had left him an ominous message right here in his office. At first he'd been determined to have the Colby Agency look into the issue. It wasn't every day that someone who knew how to best his security dropped by his office and left such a bold message.

I know what you did.

But then he'd decided to drop it. Why stir up his painful past? He knew what he had done. Why allow anyone else to delve into that unpleasant territory?

If the man who'd left him that message was trying to reach him again, he'd certainly prompted Devon's attention this time.

What better way to send a message than to resurrect the dead?

Get 4 FREE REWARDS!

We'll send you 2 FREE Books plus 2 FREE Mystery Gifts.

Harlequin® Romantic Suspense books feature heart-racing sensuality and the promise of a sweeping romance set against the backdrop of suspense.

FREE Value Over **$20**

Get 4 FREE REWARDS!

**We'll send you 2 FREE Books
<u>plus</u> 2 FREE Mystery Gifts.**

Harlequin Presents® books feature a sensational and sophisticated world of international romance where sinfully tempting heroes ignite passion.

FREE
Value Over
$20

YES! Please send me 2 FREE Harlequin Presents® novels and my 2 FREE gifts (gifts are worth about $10 retail). After receiving them, if I don't wish to receive any more books, I can return the shipping statement marked "cancel." If I don't cancel, I will receive 6 brand-new novels every month and be billed just $4.55 each for the regular-print edition or $5.55 each for the larger-print edition in the U.S., or $5.49 each for the regular-print edition or $5.99 each for the larger-print edition in Canada. That's a savings of at least 11% off the cover price! It's quite a bargain! Shipping and handling is just 50¢ per book in the U.S. and 75¢ per book in Canada*. I understand that accepting the 2 free books and gifts places me under no obligation to buy anything. I can always return a shipment and cancel at any time. The free books and gifts are mine to keep no matter what I decide.

Choose one: ☐ **Harlequin Presents®**
Regular-Print
(106/306 HDN GMYX)

☐ **Harlequin Presents®**
Larger-Print
(176/376 HDN GMYX)

Name (please print)

Address   Apt. #

City   State/Province   Zip/Postal Code

Mail to the **Reader Service:**
IN U.S.A.: P.O. Box 1341, Buffalo, NY 14240-8531
IN CANADA: P.O. Box 603, Fort Erie, Ontario L2A 5X3

Want to try two free books from another series! Call 1-800-873-8635 or visit www.ReaderService.com.
